River in the Meadow

R. SOLACE. B

River In The Meadow

Copyright © 2024 by R. Solace. B.

MILTON & HUGO L.L.C.
4407 Park Ave., Suite 5
Union City, NJ 07087, USA

Website: *www.miltonandhugo.com*
Hotline: *1- 888-778-0033*
Email: *info@miltonandhugo.com*

Ordering Information:
Quantity sales. Special discounts are granted to corporations, associations, and other organizations. For more information on these discounts, please reach out to the publisher using the contact information provided above.

Library of Congress Control Number: 2024904761
ISBN-13:   979-8-89285-026-1   [Paperback Edition]
                  979-8-89285-027-8   [Hardback Edition]
                  979-8-89285-028-5   [Digital Edition]

Rev. date: 05/30/2024

Table of Contents

Cricket Mont

Darwin Pakín

Gregory Mont

Cricket Mont Part Two

Darwin Pakín Part Two

Cricket Mont Part Three

July 16th, 1985

Representation

LGBTQ+
(Of major and minor characters)
-MLM **(Gay)** (Cricket Mont)
-WLW **(Lesbian)** (Moss Brine/ Ruby Bashwin/ Mrs. RedRoom/ Mrs. Ink)
-**Sapphic** (Lilly Petaldrop/ MariGold Poppy/ Cyrus Monroe)
-**Bisexual** (Rocket Chili/ Darwin Pakín/ Wasma Lovin)
-**Asexual** (Rocket Chili)
-**Transgender** (Moss Brine/ MariGold Poppy)
-**Demigirl** (Ruy RedInk)
-**Pansexual** (Clover Lockhilo/ Ruy RedInk)
-**Aroace** (Acorn Meg)

Physical/Mental Disabilities
-**Anxiety**
-**Blindness**
-**PPD** (Postpartum Depression)
-**Tics** (anxiety induced)

Ethnicities
-**Dominican**   -**Italian**
-**Haitian**   -**Russian**

(Fictional)
-**Fairyian**   -**Floralin**
-**Gnomian**   -**Trollian**
-**Witches**   -**Warlocks**
-**Tree Guardians** -**Pures**
-**Mushians**   -**Goddesses**

Pronunciation Guide

(Fictional places, fictional races, and character names that might be said wrong)

*Iviny (character) *I-vin-EE*
*Darwin Pakín (character) *Darwin Pa-key-nah*
*Wasma Lovin/Waszy (character) *Was-mah Love-in / Was-ie*
*Clover Lockhilo (character) *Clover Lock-hill-oh*
*Tisi (character) *Tis-see*
*Fairyian (race) *Fair-E-an*
*Floralin (race) *Floral-in*
*Gnomain (race) *Gnome-E-an*
*Trollian (race) *Troll-E-an*
*Mushian (race) *Mu-sh-E-an*
*Union Beria (race) *Union Bear-e-ah*
*Treen (fictional language) *Tree-nuh*
*Floraloxy (fictional creature) *Floral-ox-EE*

Content Warnings

-Crude language
-Violence
-Death/Death of a parent
-Mental and physical abuse
-Child abuse
-Alcohol and drug abuse
-Homophobia
-Transphobia
-Drowning
-Anxiety attacks
- Suicide
-Blood
-Strangling

To my sibling, Tyler, for everything.
I love you, big sib. Thank you so much
for helping me bring this book to life.

-R, Solace. B

The Beginning Of The Colonies

Millions and trillions of years ago, there was a flash of blue light. From light, the creation of the first Tree Guardian came into existence. The being lived alone for centuries, living in the cosmos with the stars and galaxies, until one day, he got very lonely. So, the Tree Guardian used his powers and created five other Tree Beings to live with.

Years came and went. The darkness and stars made time blend so easily. The Trees wanted something more than this, something better. That's when the idea of finding a home came about. While searching for said land, they came across a small island in the middle of an ocean. They were happy, even if it was tiny at the time. But the Tree Guardians slowly started getting bored of their new home after only a few months. Using all their powers of creation simultaneously, they expanded the island. With more space, they realized that the land was too much just for them. So, one by one, they made a new life form and set them down on the new land to call home.

The Tree Guardians put the Fairyians in the North Wing, the Gnomians in the East Wing, the Floralins and Trollians in the West Wing, and the Witches and Warlocks in the South Wing of the land. (At some point, the Trollians did migrate to the North Wing because it had huge caves.)

The oldest and the first created Tree Being thought long and hard about a name for the new territory. He'd been referring to it as 'the colonies' for a long time, which it is still called today. Name after name was thought of, but nothing stuck until one finally did. This name was *'Union Beria.'*

Now having a home, a name for their home, and creatures to live in it, the Tree Guardians made an official government. For their first steps in making a government, they created a scroll on which they wrote all the rules and laws of the land and established the center land mass of Union Beria as the home for all Tree Guardians. Over time, the Wings people gave it the name *'The Center.'* Though, The Center wasn't just for the Tree Beings. It was made to be a universal place where everyone was one with each other. No matter if you were a fish swimming in the oceans that surrounded Union Beria or if you were the oldest of Guardians, you were equal. You all worked together no matter what you were.

Magic flows through Union Beria and its inhabitants like the wind flows through hair.

Everyone knows that. Creation plays a massive part in the lives of the people and history of the colonies, and it is even spoken of in the scroll of rules and laws,

> *"...The day when we are reborn*
> *from the dirt, rock,*
> *and moss. A cycle that follows*
> *us forever till we are*
> *put to rest once again back to*
> *dirt, rock, and moss..."*

Creation isn't just making something never seen before. Sometimes, it's the realization of who you are and the rebirth of yourself.

However, over the years, something started to happen to Union Beria. *Rips* began appearing randomly from thin air, worrying the Tree Guardians to the extreme. Peering through them, it was apparent to what they were—*portal openings.* A theory started to pass through the Wings. People started to think that the more the Guardians used their powers to create anything, the more it slowly began to rip their world, exposing it to other realms.

With the fear of anyone getting hurt, the Guardians gave jobs to the strongest of beings that came in second to them, the Goddesses, the sisters of the Tree Guardians. Each Goddess was given a single portal to watch over for the rest of their lives. I wish I could tell you it was under control from there on, but it wasn't. The more magic used by the Guardians to create life, the more the magic started to seep through the ripped portals into other realms. In this case, this realm was where the Humans lived.

But this story doesn't deal with any portal or random people. It had to deal with a portal out in the woods of LongEdge, Ohio, waiting years till the right people came along.

Cricket Mont

PART ONE

Chapter 1
LongEdge

*M*y days are like every other day in the summer. I wake up when the sun rises over the hill and start on my chores immediately. Father has already gone to work by this time, so I make my way around the yard and house alone. My chores follow according to the early hours. First, I make my bed and get myself into my work overalls. Then, I go to the chickens and hens to collect their eggs and feed them. They're always so grateful for the food, and their happy clucking makes me smile. After that, I moved to the garden, picking the fresh fruits and vegetables to be harvested. My Walkman plays music in my ears as I work on the rest of my chores: sweeping, cleaning the pens, getting the mail, feeding my dog Milo and letting him out of his dog house, and more.

Time slowly rolled towards two in the afternoon as I cleaned some fresh cucumber and basil in the sink. Drying my hands off, I flipped through the mail I had collected. While doing so, I stumbled upon a letter from my best friend, Rocket. Rocket went to Russia for the summer to visit family and had been sending Moss and me letters. I love that he always tries to keep in contact with us even when he is out of the country. The three of us, Rocket, Moss, and I, have been glued at the hip for many years. Although, I've been stuck with Rocket for a little longer.

We met in the third grade after I moved from Queens to LongEdge. He was a sweet kid and very hyperactive like me, so it was easy to become his friend in seconds. We sat next to each other in class, and I knew from then on that he wasn't leaving my side. At recess, he enjoyed taking soda bottles, shaking them up, and opening the lid to make them explode everywhere. He always said the same monologue whenever doing so. He'd say that the rocket would leave the atmosphere in 3... 2... 1, and then he would let go of the top, and we'd watch it take off together. No wonder everyone gave him the nickname, 'Rocket.' He was always trying to take on NASA with his soda bottle rockets.

The only hiccup in our friendship was that we couldn't understand each other fully. Rocket didn't know how to speak English well when we first met because his parents mainly spoke Russian at home. It took us a long time to learn to communicate with one another, but once we were able to, we couldn't stop talking.

I learned a lot about him from the stories he would tell me. I know from his tales that Rocket's parents moved to the United States in the late '60s to start a new life. After settling in Ohio, Margaret, and Ivan, Rocket's mom and dad, wanted to start a family, but they had issues when trying to conceive children. They tried everything, but after so many failed attempts, they lost hope. One day, a friend of theirs told them about this adoption agency in Pennsylvania that was closing up, and the owners were trying to find families quickly for the kids. Even if they lost hope of having their own, they drove to the adoption agency to check it out. The two made eyes with a beautiful baby boy named Doug when arriving there. Those eyes were all they needed to say yes to taking him home. Doug must have been magical or a sign from the Gods to the Chili's to start trying again for a baby because three years later, Rocket was born. Margaret was so happy to have a baby boy of her own and have a family to love forever. She even calls him her miracle baby, which he enjoys bragging about. Regardless, we have been best friends for about nine years, and I couldn't ask for a better best friend. Well, other than Moss, of course.

My other best friend is named Moss Brine. Rocket and I met her in fifth grade when she was moved to the same class as us. Moss was born a boy, but that doesn't matter to me since she's happier as a girl. She has been going by Moss for years now. It's been so long that I can't even remember her old name. I have to say; she was one of the lucky ones. I remember when she came out to her parents. Her mom was so accepting of her new identity that she even gave Moss all of her old '70s clothes to wear to make her feel more comfortable in her skin. It took her dad a bit of time to fully grasp the new changes, but after some time with her staying at my house, everything became good for her at home.

Mitchel and Nadia, her parents, started homeschooling Moss two weeks into seventh grade. Why? Well, when she was walking home from school, a group of older boys chased her down the street to her home. This happened a couple of months after she changed her name and started wearing more feminine clothing. Her mom and dad went directly to the principal to report the incident, and the principal, on his high horse, did nothing to punish the perpetrators. He even called Moss by the wrong name the whole time. The situation made the Brine's sick to their stomachs. If the administrators weren't going to protect their daughter, they would. Before leaving that office that day, they had unenrolled Moss entirely out of that school. Although I don't see Moss in study hall anymore, Rocket and I can still see her after school when we go to her place to play Atari and hang out with her on the weekends when we adventure in the forest. I'm glad she is safer now that she's out of school, but what is *'safe'* in this world anymore?

I opened the letter that was from Rocket.

Dear Cricket,

Привет! (Hello!) I should be home soon, but when you read this, I think I should be on my flight back. I have many photos and ~~suevinters~~ souvenirs for you guys! Hopefully, you aren't missing my beautiful face in your lives. I'll see you as soon as I can when I'm home.

−Rocket :>

I smiled to myself as I read the letter.

"At least his grammar is improving. I didn't have to decipher it this time, so that's good. I should be happy he spelled my name right." I laugh at my dyslexic friend.

I put the letter under my arm and continued looking through the mail when, from the front of the house, I heard the door open.

"I'm home from work, Crick!" A familiar male voice yelled. The man walked into the kitchen where I was.

"Hey, Father. You're home from work early today. Is this a special occasion?" I asked my dad as he took off his shoes and tie. After doing so, he gave me a small hug.

"Your mother. She contacted me at work, and you know how she can't talk to me without an argument. I came home early to deal with her," Father sighed, "Cricket, could you go outside for a while with your music? It's an adult conversation."

I looked at his face. He looked tired and annoyed.

"Of course, Father. I was planning on reading the morning paper outside anyway." I grabbed the newspaper and my Walkman, smiling at my Father, and left the kitchen through the backdoor.

I turned my music on as I made my way to the tire swing in the backyard with my *Queen* cassette starting on track one. This happens more than I wish it did: Mama calling to complain about something. Now, I wish I was inside to see what it was about this time. It's probably about how much child support he is 'taking' from her, even though he made it super low for her to pay. Whatever it is, I enjoy the time I have to relax, even if it's on a tire swing waiting for Father to give me the okay to come back inside.

Sitting on the old swing, I grabbed the newspaper, putting my feet on the tree trunk to stop the swinging motions so I didn't feel sick while reading. Yes, most 16-year-olds don't go around reading the morning paper; at least, the kids I know don't. The only reason I even look through it is for the stories.

'*TUESDAY, JULY 16TH, 1985*', it read in bold print under the paper's name, *LongEdge Post*. I skipped through the labeled pages: *Weather, Sports, Cartoons, Town Events*, etc.

"Page 11, there you are," I said to myself, flipping through the pages carefully so they didn't rip. At the top of the page, it read '*Town Tales And Happenings*' in bold. The town I live in, LongEdge, was known for its strange events. For such a small town, it has a lot of history. I've spent many days in the public library, mainly because I volunteered there during the school year. When I have free time, though, I read books about the history of this town. It's pretty interesting, actually. LongEdge used to be a camp during the Civil War in the 1860s. Many people died on the land, of course. The tales I read range from ghost sightings to what's going on here in LongEdge that generally seems '*weird.*'

Recently, there have been these... *earthquakes.* No one understands why they have been happening. We don't even live on or near any tectonic plates.

I skim through the writing and go into the theories. People will be asked in interviews about their thoughts on what's happening. I've heard many crazy things, like the world is coming to an end, and we need to start praying for God's forgiveness. Usually, I'll chuckle at the thought. People really do think that the end is near. But still, I read them, probably out of pity for the person. Anyway, theories are theories, and nothing is fact until proven. But nothing can explain anything going on. I've seen weird trucks rush through our town on many occasions. They always head in the same direction, but no one knows why.

Personally, I think something is happening that isn't good. Father and I have talked about all of this many times, and he even agrees that something isn't right. It makes sense for him to have these doubts. Before I was born, he worked for our government, the Army, but was dismissed from duty to be there for my childhood. I've always wondered if he would return if given the chance to. However, he said he hated the work he was told to do and preferred to work a regular, 'mediocre desk job.' Anyway, I have this feeling whenever we talk about the earthquakes and the trucks, as if my gut is trying to tell me something. I have no clue why, though.

I was still reading the paper when I heard my name called. "Cricket! It's time to come inside now." I looked down at my watch; it read 3:54 p.m.

"It was just two o'clock, like five seconds ago?" I was puzzled as I walked back to the house, lowering my music, which was starting on track six now.

Father put food on my plate as I walked in from the back door. We usually ate dinner early, as Father grew up doing so. I took my shoes off and sat down. Father always made dinner fun, even if it was just us. We talk about everything and anything that comes to mind.

"What did you read about today, Sport?" Father asked me.

I looked up at Father's eyes. His dark curls covered his forehead, and some stubble had started to regrow on his lower face. He was wearing his standard gray button-up uniform from work, and his glasses were sliding down his nose. We have the same eyes, the same type of hair, the same skin tone, the same freckles, and even the same white pieces of hair; it's just that his are caused by old age and mine I was born with.

"Well, the same stuff. Mr. Lin *lost* his dog again," I replied, shoving food in my mouth.

"Oh, that poor old man. His dementia isn't getting better. That rat of a dog died two years ago," Father replied under his breath.

"Father! Don't say that," I argued.

"Okay, okay, I'm sorry," he grinned.

"Anyway," I rolled my eyes at him, "there still hasn't been anything about the earthquakes. I wonder how long it will take for a reasonable answer."

"Well, reasonable? Never. An answer people will probably just take because they wish it were over already, maybe in a couple of months? I bet they already know and don't want to panic the townsfolk. Some days I'm happy I left that shit show. There was just too much drama. They even tried calling me a while ago to see if they can bribe my way back as *'Commander Mont.'*" He used his silly voice when saying that name, which always makes me chuckle.

"And what did they want you back for?" I asked innocently.

Father looked at his plate and picked up his fork, putting mashed potatoes in his mouth, "Nothing, you need to worry about Cricket because I said no."

Father was lying, of course. I can tell when he does. His eyebrows lift, he scrunches his face, and he doesn't make eye contact. That's what I do when I lie too. But I don't tell him I know he is lying because I don't need Father to be mad at me, even though he could never be angry at me. His voice sounded dry, and it didn't help that he had been yelling at Mama earlier. Why did he have to hide the reason they wanted him back?

"Oh, okay," I picked at my food, feeling awkward that I had asked.

After a second of silence, I spoke up again, "So what did Mama want?"

No matter what I said, the air in the room felt tense. He looked up at me. His eyes were a bit glassy, but I didn't want him to realize I could see that.

"Oh, well," he started to say, " the phone call with your mother. It's just—actually, it's not important right now, but after dinner or later, she wants you to call her." Father's voice was low, sounding defeated.

"It's okay, Father. I understand. Mama is... something else, " I tried to joke. I saw a slight lift of his lips but nothing more. "And whatever she tries to tell me in her drunken state, you know I don't have much of a heart for her anymore."

"Cricket, I *know*, but it's a little different this time."

I just looked at him. What did he mean by that?

Chapter 2
That Night I Left

*I*t took me a while to get the courage to call Mama. What was she going to tell me? Usually, I don't take whatever she says to heart, but seeing Father so distraught today worries me. He always puts a smile on for me, even when it is terrible. It must mean that anything Mama will tell me might be something to take seriously.

I slowly picked up the telephone from the wall and dialed her number.

It rings.

"Hello? Mama?" I held the phone up to my ear.

"Cricket, it's good to hear your voice again. How long has it been? Two months?" Her voice was raspy, like usual. It doesn't help that she smokes like a chimney.

"Eh, more like two years," I grumbled over the phone while my fingers twirled with the spiral telephone cord.

"It couldn't have been *that* long, Cricket."

Was she being serious? The last time she called or wanted to talk to me was Christmas of '83. Even then, she called me drunk, and Father had to take over the phone.

"Anyway, Father said you had something to tell me? Sounds more important than this conversation about you trying to remember the last time you called to talk to me like a real mother would." The cold-hearted words left my lips. Even if I wanted to take them back, I can't, but I don't plan on doing so.

"Oh, I guess your father has rubbed his sarcastic tone on you too," her voice broke to a whisper for a second, "That son-of-a-bitch... but yes, there is something important for me to tell you!" I could hear the pour of something into a glass cup with ice over on her line. I won't be surprised if it was some scotch.

Trying to gloss over the fact she called my father such a vulgar name, my grip on the phone was getting tighter. "And what would that be, Mama?" The thought of hanging up on her got stronger with every word that came out of her mouth.

"Well, you remember James, right? My boyfriend?" Mama asked me.

"Which one was that? I can only remember Charlie and Austin."

"No, those relationships are over. James, James McLee? The banker? Well, he proposed! And I, as your mother, want you to come back to Queens for the wedding! You can start to grow a relationship with him. He even has two kids, one of whom is your age. You will have siblings and everything. Doesn't that sound fun?" I could feel that she was smiling because of her tone.

"Are you being serious? Are you asking me to be a part of some family I don't even know?" I punctuated certain words.

"Oh, come on, Cricket, don't be a prick about this. You will meet Olivia and Noah and even make some new friends while you are here. We both know the friends you have now aren't good for you."

How could she say that? She doesn't even know them like I do. Even if it's the alcohol talking, she still said it.

"Excuse me, but they *are* good for me. *They* have been there through the bad and good days, unlike you. I don't wish to be a part of *any* family of yours. You couldn't even

16

take care of me. How could you care for James' kids? I don't even know them, and I think they don't deserve to have a mother as neglectful as you, let alone know you." The words flowed from my mouth. Years of anger I never knew was there and never being seen as a child of hers spilled out of me.

Mama wasn't done yet with me, though. I could feel the heat of fury through the phone. "I am your mother! You do *NOT* speak to me in such a vulgar way. I gave you life! I brought you into this world, and I can take you out of it!" She threatens.

"Have fun trying when you live five hundred miles away."

Silence took over the conversation; it spoke words so loudly it made the room feel small.

"Cricket, I understand you're upset, but the date is final. You are coming to Queens tomorrow night via plane. You better start packing. You're staying here for the rest of the summer."

My eyes widened in shock, "My 17th birthday is on the 18th, which is in two days. Are you telling me I must miss my birthday to be with you and not with the people who care for me?!" I yelled back.

"It is final, Cricket. I will see you soon. I love you."

Love is a strong word. It should be used when you truly love someone, not when you try to force them to love you back.

"Goodbye, Catherine," I hung up the phone before she could say anything back.

My temper was through the roof. I started to pace the kitchen, hands on my head. Father came into the room with a gentle approach.

"Cricket-" he began to say.

"Why didn't you tell me that I'm forced to be with that *WITCH* for the rest of the summer?!" All I felt was the fire in my body that wouldn't burn out so quickly.

"I'm sorry, Sport. I tried to stop her; believe me, I tried, but she was inflamed with pride because the courts told her she could see you once she was getting help with the drug problem. Honestly, I thought she would have never remembered that was a part of the deal. I thought she would have drank her memory away by now," Father tries to defend himself.

"I wish she could have forgotten about me altogether. I wish I could forget her and all she has ever said. I wish she could leave us alone. I don't want a new family. You are my family. Rocket and Moss are my family. Hell, even their families are my family. Not her drunk-ass. It doesn't matter if I have her DNA or if she has a new shiny ring from a guy with two kids who would rather have a plant as a brother than me!" My eyes got blurry with tears. I couldn't stop them from pouring. The tears burned my skin as if my face was on a hot stove. "I don't want to go, Father. Please tell me I don't have to go," I pleaded with him, wiping my face with my hands, "She doesn't even like me."

I felt Father's arms quickly pull me in. He would be like charcoal if the fire inside me could burn him.

"Cricket..." he started to say, but his voice struggled as he choked back tears. "She does like you. It's just that she sees you as *different*. Your mother grew up in a different time, with different ideas of *normal*."

"Normal! Being there for your child is normal. Drinking and smoking your life away because your child is *different* isn't normal! Even Moss's dad was more accepting when she opened up to him. But my own mother- she'd rather try to beat the queer out of me instead. Hoping it was like a cold and go away. That's not normal!" I pushed him away with my hands, shouting, not at him but at the world. All I want is to be heard by someone, anyone who is willing to listen. "And I don't need pity from you or anyone for that matter." My voice became lower; my throat hurt from yelling.

Father looked at me with worry and tears in his eyes. I've never broken down like this, not even when I was agitated. I tried to walk away, but Father grabbed my arm. "That is not true, Cricket. I don't pity you."

"That's bullshit, and this whole thing is bullshit!" I ripped my arm away from him and ran to my room, locking my door.

"Cricket Andrew Mont, can we please just talk?" Father raised his voice as he followed me to my door, jiggling the doorknob.

"I'm going to bed. Please, just leave me alone," I told him, wiping my tears with my arm. I needed some time to think, to be alone.

After a second or two, I heard him sigh and leave down the hallway. The light in the hallway that appeared from under my door also shut off. I sat on my bed, holding my pillow to my face as I bawled my eyes out of my head. That lasted for a while till the only thing I could feel was the pain in my heart— the feeling of a gasoline-covered heart that someone put a match to.

An hour or so goes by, and the clock reads nine-thirty at night. The house was quiet, and the only sounds were of the real crickets outside.

I thought to myself, *I can't stay in this house anymore. I need to get out, or I might not be able to later.*

Looking at my desk, I grab my Walkie-Talkie and go to the normal channel where my friends and I speak.

"Hello? Hello?" I say over the line, then sigh, "This is... 'Camel Cricket.' Over."

"Camel Cricket Man! How are you? I'm home from Russia if you can't tell. Did you miss me? Over," a loud voice spoke from the other side with a Russian accent. It was Rocket!

We all used code names, if you can even call them that. Rocket's was Rocket Man, Moss's was Mossie Mow, and mine was Camel Cricket, sadly.

"I guess you could say that. Over." My eyes shot over to the corkboard where all the letters, drawings, literally anything Rocket and Moss gave me were. Even the plethora of polaroids of all three of us on my desk can answer that question for Rocket. Why wouldn't I have missed him?

"Why are you calling now? 'Tis late? Over," he slurs his words.

"It's been a rough night. Is Mossie Mow connected? Over," I replied to the Russian boy.

"Yes, I am! Sorry, my mom was tightening my braids. I am all ears now. Over," Moss spoke in a soft voice.

"It's a big ask, but can we see each other right now? It's really important. Over." The sound in my voice was pain that even they could hear.

"Oh, um, sure! I'd have to sneak out, though. Over," Moss said first.

"Same here, but no problem!-" Rocket began to say, as his mother cut him off.

[1]"С кем ты разговариваешь?" asked Mrs. Chili to Rocket in Russian.

"Ugh, sorry. Give me one second, guys. [2]Мама, я слушаю тебя-" his line goes silent.

I hear Moss giggle, "He is always getting in trouble for something. Anyway, I'll come to see you. I'll force Rocket to bike me over since mine is still getting repairs. Over."

As she spoke, I threw some items in an old backpack, like water and a flashlight.

---

[1] С кем ты разговариваешь?: Who are you talking to? (*S kem ty razgovarivayesh'?*)

[2] Мама, я слушаю тебя: Mom, I am listening (*Mama, ya slushayu tebya*)

"Ah, [3]Да it is cool with me. Be there in fifteen! OVER!" Rocket yells over the line.

"Okay, great. Meet me by the old car. Over and out," I whisper, turning my Walkie-Talkie off and putting it in my bag. Slowly, I opened my window. I was surprisingly small enough to fit through it with ease. Before I left, though, I put a note on my desk.

> *'Father, I needed to go somewhere where I could breathe. I promise I'm safe. I hope you aren't mad. If anything, I'll probably end up at Rocket's house.*
>
> *-Cricket'*

I signed the letter, put it on my desk under a rock, then climbed out of my window.

---

[3] Да: Yes (*da*)

Chapter 3
The Portal

The sky was getting darker each minute I waited by the old car. This car I talk of is a secret spot where my friends and I hang out. We have a vast forest in the backyard on my father's property. One day, the three of us were walking through the forest when we came across an old car that had to be from the 1940s. From that day forward, it was the spot we all went to when we needed to get away from things, like my mother in this case.

A bright light flashed towards me from a little distance away. It was Rocket and Moss on a bike. Moss used her flashlight to help guide Rocket to our spot, as he probably would have hit a tree without it.

"Hey guys, over here," I whisper-yelled to them.

Rocket propped the bike up against a tree, "We are alone. There is no need to whisper. Why did you want us to come here? I had to lie to my mother and say I'd be sleeping at your house."

Moss cut in after Rocket's comment, "I'm happy your dog didn't start barking at us like he normally does. Cane Corso's are loud as hell." She came up to me and gave me a small hug like usual, her long blond braids scratching against my face. She was right about my dog, though. He barks at a leaf blowing sometimes, so I'm happy he didn't make a sound tonight.

Rocket slid into the passenger seat of the old car. I sat behind the rusted wheel, and Moss followed into the backseat, the doors creaking at the hinges.

"So, what is it? Are you okay?" Moss looked over at me.

"Well." My eyes moved from Moss and then to Rocket, meeting his eyes. His doe gray eyes sparkled from the moonlight. Looking him up and down, I could tell he hadn't brushed his hair. His curly, very choppy red and black mullet was a rat's nest, and his earrings were caught in the curls. His clothes were all wrinkled, as if he tossed them on himself from his floor, which he did often enough. He wore layers of black clothes and had a leather jacket with multiple patches littering it and a raven painting on the backside. Rocket even had his nails painted black, and his fingers were covered in many rings. The boy I look at I admire with a passion, one that could be seen as romantic. A crush, maybe. Though, I doubt he would like me back.

I started to tell them what happened. The words poured from my lips like a waterfall. With each waterfall drip, Moss and Rocket's faces became crossed with sadness.

"Cricket, I'm so sorry that happened! Wait, does that mean you're leaving us?" Moss asked frantically, panic rising in her voice.

"Hell no! That's why I came here," I paused, taking a breath, "I want to run away so I don't have to leave tomorrow. They can't force someone to go somewhere if you can't find them."

Their eyes got wide. "Dude, are you serious?!" Rocket began.

"You can't just run. What about your dad? What about us?" Moss finished the Russian boy's sentence.

"He was just going to let Catherine take me. Why would I stay if he will just comply with her?" I told them.

Moss looked at me with anxious hazel eyes, "Where would you go? The first place he would look is our houses."

"I can stay here, in the forest," I said.

"You forget coyotes are things out here," Rocket points out.

"Guys, I don't know right now. I just don't know what to do," I wallowed to my friends. "This is so unfair. Why does she want to be in my life NOW?! She had so many opportunities to, you know, love me as her son and be a good mom." My face was getting hot with anger, and my sight blurred from tears.

I felt hands grab my face, finding Rocket staring back at me. "Hey, there's no need to cry. We could," he started to think and paused as he looked around. "...Follow me," Rocket continued, letting go of my face and leaving the old car. Moss and I met each other's gaze, confused, but soon followed after him with our flashlights on.

"Rocket, where are you going? It's too late to be adventuring out here alone. We just talked about coyotes, remember? I don't want to be eaten today!" Moss pronounced most of her words like you would see drama kids act out scenes on stage. While she spoke, she kept looking over her shoulder for any coyote-shaped movement and shadows.

"If Cricket stays here, then we will stay with him," he says confidently.

"Have you been smoking pot?! You must be high off your tits if you think that's a good idea," she replied to him with a dumbfounded expression.

"Definitely," he jokes, turning around to shoot a smirk our way. He's such an idiot.

The sky's darkness grew around each tree as we took each step. Moss had taken Rocket's arm as I walked on the other side of her. I looked over at Rocket from my side, which was slightly blocked by Moss's frame. While watching him, I could tell that Rocket looked so comfortable with Moss's arm around him. He once mentioned having a crush on her growing up, but I haven't asked for my own sake in a while. He had a crush on her from before she transitioned. Even now, I don't know if he liked the boy version of her or always saw the girl within her. No matter what his reasoning was for liking Moss, I feel something profound in my chest whenever I remember Rocket's confession, and I feel that way now when they're walking next to each other with their arms linked. Sadness? Jealousy? I don't know, but it hurts me for some reason. We are all friends who occasionally flirt platonically, so why am I feeling this way? Anyway, I have other things to worry about right now.

The flashlights guide our steps in the deep forest. I knew the forest like the back of my hand, but something was different. We left the car, going right. There should be an ivy fence around this area like there always was, but nothing was there when I checked over my shoulder.

"Hey, did we pass the fence already?" I questioned my friends.

"Most likely? I wasn't paying much attention to it. I'm too scared to care right now. This forest is scary at night," Moss replied, clutching onto both mine and Rocket's arms now, her eyes blown wide in slight fear.

Even with the flashlights, seeing anything in the thick woods was hard. The lights stopped us from tripping on overgrown roots but couldn't penetrate the darkness. I moved the light onto my watch to check the time, but something was wrong. The clock hand wasn't moving, and the hands' clicking sound was silent.

"What the hell? How long have we been out here?" I stop walking for a second. I looked down at the watch as my friends turned back to look at me.

"Twenty minutes? I'm not counting. I'm, you know, trying not to guide us to our deaths," Rocket said, pointing the flashlight at my face.

"Is that necessary?" I covered my eyes from the light.

[4]"Да, now what?" Rocket had a hand on his hip, adding too much sass for a moment like this. He was a jokester, though, in and out.

"My watch, it stopped clicking. It's brand new, so I don't get why it's not working," I told them.

"Well, my watch says 10:01 pm. Your watch must have broken. You probably hit it while doing your chores," Moss nudged our arms to keep walking.

They shrugged it off, but it stayed in my head as we walked. It just doesn't make sense.

The forest felt like it would never end, as if time was taking its sweet time moving forward. I can't believe Rocket is making us walk around the forest at night like this. Yes, it was my idea to come out here, but I wasn't planning on walking so late. I still haven't seen the ivy fence.

As we continued walking, more time passed. My legs ached as they grew exhausted since I'd been up and going all day. That's when I noticed that our flashlights started to flicker. I patted mine, knowing that sometimes the battery flakes, but my flashlight kept blinking

---

[4] Да: Yes (*da*)

its light until it fully turned off. I looked at my friends and watched their lights act the same way.

"Ugh! Come on, you stupid piece of crap!" Moss banged her light on her hand.

We stopped walking because Moss had lost her cool. She continued to bang the flashlight more. Rocket took it from her, "It won't help to bring it back! Now stay close," Rocket slowly started to inch forward again. A minute could not have gone by before we heard leaves begin to crackle and whoosh behind us. We all froze with panic.

"Don't move, and stay quiet," I whispered.

Moss was panicking a lot more now, holding her hands in a fist. "I promised myself I didn't want to die with you guys here with me." The panic again was adamant in her voice, making it crack a bit.

"Wow, so nice of you. Thanks," Rocket replied sarcastically.

"Shut up, the both of you," I told them.

We waited, hoping not to hear anything else in the silent world. Moss was the first to break it.

"Look over there. I see a light. I say we should book it," Moss suggested.

It was a great idea, even in my worried state. "Okay, let's do it on a count of three. One," I began.

[5]"Два," Rocket said next in Russian.

"Three," Moss began to say as we ran to the light as quickly as we could, dropping our flashlights as we fled. It didn't matter to us. It's not like they would work anyway.

We didn't stop running until we crossed into the lit area. The closer we got, the clearer everything became. When our bodies passed through the light, it felt like we ran into a giant spider web, though there wasn't one there. What a weird feeling it was.

"Did we really hike until morning? My Gods, my mom's going to kill me when I get home." Moss spoke, out of breath from running.

"Note: Don't wear jeans when you need to run," Rocket huffed. His hands were pressed on his knees as he caught his breath.

"What is this place?" Moss asked aloud.

---

[5] Два: Two (*dva*)

I took a second to look around, stepping into a patch of flowers. This place was foreign to me. It was a beautiful meadow filled with many flowers, but most were *Forget Me Nots*. The sight was words more than beautiful can explain, maybe *magnificent?* Moss was happy to see brightly colored flowers and went into the field, picking some and putting them in her braids. So much was happening that my brain couldn't keep up with me. My eyes traced the very tall trees, the bright flowers of different sizes, a log bench that looked handmade, and a peaceful river that flowed right next to it. I sat on the bench, looking at the water.

"I've never seen this place before. Where are we?" I picked a rock up, skipping it on the river.

"Maybe I could help you." A voice that wasn't Rocket, Moss, or I spoke up. The voice was deep but still feminine, with a slight accent.

All of us looked around, "Who's there?" Rocket yelled out.

"No need to shout, children. I'm right here," the voice said.

We looked where it came from to see a lady peering behind the trees. When she revealed herself to us, she was gorgeous. Her hair was in light blue locs, and she had a green and purple beaded necklace around her neck. She was wearing a sheer blue robe with a turquoise dress underneath. As we looked closer, her eyes were pale white, which popped out from her dark-rich skin. The woman came closer to us. With a massive smile, she was feeling her way through the flowers, making her way to the river's edge. I looked at my friends. Rocket's face was contorted in confusion, and Moss looked at the woman in awe. I could see Moss's hazel eyes not leaving her. The woman knelt by the river bank, placing her hand over the water.

"Excuse me, Miss?" Moss's voice was soft, like usual, but nervous, which was explainable even for her.

"Yes, my dear? What is it?" The woman continued to face the river.

"Where are we exactly?" Moss asked.

"Well, you're in my home. It's been so long since I had visitors," the woman replied.

"Oh. Well, we are sorry to intrude on your beautiful home," Moss looked at me, handing the invisible talking stick over.

"Wait, this is your home? You live in the forest behind my house?" I finally spoke up.

"Technically, but we aren't near your home, dear." The woman's words made my stomach drop a bit. If we weren't in the forest behind my home, where were we? "I can promise you that you are in a safe place. No animals you have in your realm can come beyond the flower point, well, at least the vicious ones. Your little wild hares love to come and nibble on the plants here."

My eyes quickly looked over to the area we entered. The light hit the spot so perfectly that I could see a warp as if there was an invisible barrier.

I questioned the woman, "Who are you, and what is this place?"

"Well, I can answer that easily, child. My name is *Mourn*, spelled with a 'U.' I am the protector of this place. Most consider me a *Goddess*," the woman, Mourn, with a 'U' told us. "You don't have to trust me or my words. Understandably, you are afraid. You don't even know me, but even if you don't, I know you all."

Rocket moved a bit closer to the so-called Goddess Mourn. "How do you know about us?" Rocket spoke out.

"Oh, my children, there will be many things to know and questions to answer. If you can trust me enough, I will answer them all for you, but it might take some time," Mourn replied ominously.

My friends looked at me as if I had to decide what to say next. "What? How do you expect me to reply to that?" I shrugged my shoulders. All I was answered with was Moss rolling her eyes at me, and her body language shifting.

"Says the one that 'had the balls' to stay in the forest so he could run away from his problems," Moss jabbed at me, crossing her arms.

"That was a low blow, Moss. What did I even do? I wasn't the one who started wandering in the woods at night!" I stabbed back.

"Oi, ⁶Пошёл на хуй! You called us!" Rocket cursed at me.

We all just started bickering until Mourn called for us to stop. Of course, we stopped out of respect for the Goddess.

"Now, children, come sit with me for a moment, and I will explain everything to you," Mourn waved her hand, motioning us to sit with her as she moved to make more space for us.

---

⁶ Пошёл на хуй!: Fuck you! (*Poshol na khuy!*)

Moss was the first to rush over to sit right next to Mourn. Rocket and I sat beside each other, facing the other two, almost making a semi-circle. There was an awkward moment of silence. I didn't mean to start an argument with my friends. It was infrequent for us to ever get into fights because one of us always came up with a solution.

"Alright, first, which of you is sitting to my left?" Mourn asked.

"I am. My name is Moss, and these are my friends Rocket and Cricket. They are sitting on your other side. Cricket is the other sitting next to you, and Rocket is sitting at the end," Moss explained to the Goddess.

Mourn nodded, taking Moss's hand, and carefully put her hand on her face, "Such beautiful features, darling," Mourn told her.

"How can you tell? Well, your eyes..." Moss didn't know how to word it.

"I can see with my hands. With my sight gone, I have a more heightened ability with my other senses. I can feel all the details on your face. Even if I cannot see you, I can tell you are a beautiful—" Mourn felt down her chin to the middle of her neck. "-young girl."

Moss smiled brightly at the complaint. Usually, most would notice the small bump on her neck and realize what it was, but Mourn didn't seem to care.

"Now, where is this Rocket boy? I guess you were the one that was using swear words," she asked for Rocket.

Rocket leaned closer, and Mourn put her hand on his face like she did with Moss. "How did you know I was cursing?" Rocket wondered.

"I've met millions of people and know hundreds of languages. Also, your accent is ever noticeable to the ears, [7]Забавный мальчик."

"I get that a lot. But my name is Keith. Rocket is my nickname," Rocket laughed.

Mourn hummed to herself, "Mm, that's good to know. My boy, you have such strong masculine features. Oh, and this hair! My child, it is well knotted, but you have amazing curls!" She laughed a bit at the end with a huge smile.

Rocket also started to laugh a bit when she mentioned his hair. "I had no time to brush my hair when I was on the plane," he told her.

---

[7] Забавный мальчик: Funny boy (*Zabavnyy mal'chik*)

Taking her hand off his face, she faced me. Even if she couldn't see me, she definitely sensed me.

"And you must be Cricket. What unique names you all have," her hand on my face now.

"We all have some unique parents that named us," I joked with a small smile.

Her hand was very soft, and she smelt like salt water. Even though I didn't know this lady, she made me feel like I'd known her for years. Her voice was soothing, like a waterfall on a windless morning.

"That smile of yours—it feels so bright. You're so pure at heart, aren't you?" Mourn stopped and continued, "Why would you be out in your realm's forest at this time of night?"

I looked at the ground and started to fidget with my hand, "My mom wants to take me from my dad for the rest of the summer, for my birthday and everything. I thought she couldn't take me if I weren't home, so I ran. Then I told Rocket and Moss to meet me in the forest because I didn't want to be alone. I just didn't think about what I was doing. I'm sorry, guys."

Moss and Rocket smiled at me. "It's alright, Cricket. You were scared. We would have done the same if we were in your shoes.

I'm sorry for snapping at you. You were right; it was a low blow," Moss said.

Mourn sighed, "Ah, well, I'm happy you apologized, Cricket, but this is a tough situation." She looked up at the bright sky. "I don't know, as a parent myself, what I'd do if my child ran away. Well, if she could."

"You have a child?" Rocket asked.

"I do, and she's right before us," Mourn told us.

We looked around, but no one else was there. Then the Goddess moved her hand upward, and as she did, the water lifted in front of her.

"Children, I want you to meet my child," Mourn smiled at the water. The water started to move around as if it was waving to us.

"Woah, that's so cool!" Rocket said with excitement.

Mourn replied, "She is alive, just like you children. My daughter *Tisi* is so much more than a river, though. She is a portal, and I am her protector."

"I'm still confused. How is Tisi alive?" I questioned Mourn.

"Portal? How is she a portal, Mourn?" Rocket asked as well.

"We come from a place where magic is everywhere; our protectors are Tree Beings, and Trollians live in caves. A place where Fairyians, Floralins, Gnomians, Witches, and Warlocks live in peace in a colony of islands. Where there are other magical creatures like Mushians, Floraloxies, and so much more! It was my home once, long ago, but now this is my home," Mourn's words flowed out of her like it was said millions of times before. "I am the protector of the portal, my daughter. I am a Goddess, but also the *River Guardian*."

We sat with her in silence as she spoke. It was a lot to take in. Is she telling us a story, or is she telling us the truth? Magic is something that was made from capitalism, so dumb people spent money to watch someone get cut in half at a circus. But she doesn't seem to be lying.

"You didn't answer Rocket's question about the portal, and now I have so many more questions!" Moss's voice was filled with excitement.

Rocket nodded his head in response to what she said. "[8]Да, can you explain more, please? We want to know more," he begged.

---

[8] Да: Yes (*da*)

Mourn paused. She put her hand on her chin with a smile, just like I do when I try to plan something out in my head. " I can show you if you would like. Hopefully, that would answer your questions," Mourn got up from the ground as she waited for a reply.

We looked at each other. "Is this a good idea?" Rocket mouthed to Moss and me.

"There's only one way to see, I guess," Moss said, rising from the ground, and Rocket and I followed.

"Darling Tisi, open the portal, please," Mourn asked the river politely. The water started to get taller, making a circular shape. As the water rose, the ground began shaking like an *earthquake*. As she did, Tisi started to splash us a bit for fun. "Oh, knock it off, Tisi," Mourn told her daughter. The reflection of the water started to warp. Mourn grabbed our hands, "Keep your hands all locked together and close your mouth and eyes. Walking through the portal is like jumping into a body of water. It can be a bit breathtaking," Mourn giggled to herself.

When Tisi opened the portal fully, Mourn led us. We followed her instructions; I held my breath and closed my eyes tight. I'm scared. What if something happens? What if we are walking into something dangerous? What if we can't get back home,

what if,
       what if,
             what if,
                  what if...

Then I felt something tighten my hand; it was Rocket's hand in mine. There would be no more what-ifs. I had him, and he would make sure I was okay.

Chapter 4
Union Beria

*W*hen we went through the portal, it felt like we were walking through thin, wet plastic wrap. It only took seconds for us to reach the other side of wherever the portal was taking us.

"You may now open your eyes and breathe," Mourn told us.

I took a deep breath, opening my eyes.

"Woah, what the fu-" Rocket began to say before Moss covered his mouth.

"Ew! Did you lick my hand? You're so gross!" Moss shouted at Rocket, wiping her hand on his jacket.

"Dis' place is beautiful," Rocket began to say.

"More like marvelous," Moss spun around, wanting to look everywhere. Then she knelt beside the river, "It's cool that you could teleport people like that, Tisi! Fist bump?" She held her fist out as the water lifted and hit her hand back. "We are going to be great friends," Moss continued to talk to Tisi as Rocket and I continued to look around the place.

Even though we had entered the portal, it was as if the meadow followed us through. Rows of flowers and plants I'd never seen surrounded our every side. The sun shined brightly beyond the tall trees' line and into our eyes. Just looking at everything felt like I was dreaming. The meadow seemed brighter here, more colorful and vivid in life.

"So, what is this place exactly? I know you explained it, but it still doesn't make sense how it's here. We were just in the forest in my backyard moments ago," I turned to Mourn.

"This is *Union Beria*, or at least a sub-part of it. Union Beria is home to all magical creatures. Your forest is where the portal has been kept for millions of years. I can't fully give the portal's exact time and date of creation, though." The Goddess paused, then sighed.

"Children, there is a reason why I have come to you three. Recently there has been a problem. An attack has started on the people and protectors of Union Beria. Oh, the horrors. The yells and screams that I heard that used to be laughter. It's all gone. Those Humans are monsters." Mourn continued to explain, lowering her voice.

"Humans? But we are humans," Moss looked confused.

"Well, that's why I came to you, actually," Mourn moved through the flowers to stand before us. "There are more portals all over your realm, and Humans have infiltrated some of them. At first, they were peaceful, but then they started to want more from us here. Humans took control in the South Wing of the colonies before we could have stopped them. They are stationed everywhere. They have killed so many of my brothers, sisters, and siblings. But you are different. You are *special*."

Her words started to click in my head. Knowing there are more portals in our world, and most likely more in our town... it makes sense why we have been having those earthquakes recently.

"What makes us special? Why would you come to us, Goddess?" Rocket questioned her.

Mourn approached Rocket and grabbed his hand, "I was told by my superiors, the Tree Guardians, to get you." Her hand hovered over his palm, and a few seconds later, Rocket yelped.

"Ouch! [9]Какого черта?!" Rocket cried out in Russian.

Then the woman moved to Moss, grabbing her hand as well, "I've been waiting for you three for so very long, at least ever since the Humans came. I just needed a way to get all three of you here together. When I saw you coming this way, I knew it was my time."

Just like Rocket, Moss cried in pain, "Damn it! That hurt!"

The Goddess then approached me. Whatever she was doing hurt my friends, so I kept my hands away from her. That didn't stop her, though. Out of nowhere, the flowers around me grew tall, grabbed my arm, and held it out for Mourn.

"My children, the people of Union Beria require your help. Because our worlds are so close to each other due to the portals, some magical things from here can come into your world. Sometimes, children are born that are blessed by our world. Those children are called *Pures*, and you three, Moss, Rocket, and Cricket, are Pures yourselves," Mourn said.

The pain felt as if she was burning my hand with her own. I howled out, "Ow! You are hurting me!"

---

[9] Какого черта?!: What the heck?! (*Kakogo cherta?!*)

After yelling at her, she let go of me, as did the flowers. I looked down at my hand. A symbol was branded on my palm. It was a *cricket*. Of course, it was.

"What did you do to us?" Moss spoke loudly.

"You burned us like cattle!" Rocket said.

"As a Pure, you need a 'key' to open the 'door' of your blessed power that was given to you. All I did was open it by giving you the symbol. Rocket, you have a *raven*. From what I've been told, they are intelligent birds. They are said to be timeless and have truths hidden within, a form of transformation in life, I suppose. Moss, your symbol is a *sunflower*. Sunflowers have been said to bring happiness into people's lives just by sight alone," Mourn paused as she turned her head in my direction, "Cricket, your symbol is... well, a cricket, but for good reason. They are known for being blind to the world and always jumping forward first, even when in danger."

"What do these even mean? You're not making any sense," I asked the Goddess.

"That's what it means to be a raven, a sunflower, a cricket. If you can pity me for a minute, I will explain," she cleared her throat, "When describing someone as a raven, you are telling them they are good leaders, intelligent beings, and make room to allow themselves to transform in life no matter what time. Sunflowers describe someone who is a devoted person, a caring, loving, and happy individual. For crickets, well, I already explained it to you."

Of course, the mark she gave me was a cricket. I could never get away from this *stupid* name and that *stupid* bug.

I thought about each word she said to us. If she is comparing us to these things, it *is* true, all of it. Moss is the happiest and most devoted person I know. She always keeps high spirits. The world could be burning around us, and she'd be there to ensure we were doing okay. Rocket, though not always the smartest (he is his own type of smart), has been a form of leader in general. He always made sure to be on the front lines. If that means confronting bullies or being the wall between the police and the people during a protest, he always makes sure to help others. When it comes to me, it's true, too. I never think before I do most things. A perfect example is when I ran away.

Was Mourn telling us we are like her? A magical being? As if! I can't even get away from bullies at school. How could I be something so special as a Pure? Is this what she means by *blessed power*? The more she tells us, the more rabbit holes it makes me jump into.

Rocket and I started to question her trustworthiness. She did brand us, after all. Why would we trust someone who hurt us without explaining first?

Moss looked over at Rocket and then at me, "Guys, I don't think she's lying," she began to say. "She wasn't lying about the portal or whatever this place is. Just look beyond the trees! I don't think it's too far-fetched to say we might be special here. For crying out loud, did anyone ever really think we were normal in our realm?"

She was right, but when wasn't she? What Mourn talks about, about us being Pures, would make sense. Ever since we were kids, we have never fit in normally in LongEdge. We would read comic books at lunch and draw ourselves as superheroes as the other kids played ball. Growing up, we were all bullied to the point of hiding when we saw certain kids during our break periods. It definitely got worse when we got into high school. Moss was lucky never to get the second hand of public-school assholes. The memories of being shoved into lockers, being chased, becoming a literal punching bag, and worse always come to mind. Rocket would stick up for me, but that would lead to detention a lot for beating the crap out of them. The only thing Moss had to look out for was when she went into town. She was never really alone, though. Rocket and I would always be with her when we hung out in town.

And when we weren't there, she was always protected when with her family. However, she knows how to fight even when we aren't around. Moss has and will roundhouse anyone who looks at her funny.

"You're right, Moss. I'm just a bit upset with the burning of a cricket in the palm of my hand!" I replied loudly at the end.

"Sorry about that, dear. There just wasn't any other way I could do it," Mourn apologized for hurting us, and we accepted the apology.

"You told us you have been waiting for us?" Rocket pandered.

"Ah yes, thank you for reminding me. As I said, Union Beria is under attack and slowly forming into a one-sided war. We need all the help we can get to stop this 'war.' As you are technically a part of this realm, we need your help. We have a group that already knows that you are coming here. These other children need your help to save Union Beria," Mourn explains.

"Are you seriously asking us to fight in a war? We aren't even the right age to enlist in the Army, and you need us to fight in a war?" My voice shook as I worried.

"Cricket, I know this sounds terrifying, but we need allies and you to join the others. I gave you the symbols to unlock a power within the three of you," Mourn tries to reassure.

"These powers, are they like superhero powers?" Moss asked.

"Yes! I don't know what your powers entail, but they have to deal with your mark now that I gave them to you," Mourn paused. "I will give you three time to go over a plan on what you want to do. I understand if you don't wish to continue and want to go home." Mourn went over to the bench and sat down to wait.

We all looked over at each other. This was a huge decision to make at our age. We all knew the choices: either we leave, and this war of theirs fails, we stay and help them win this war, or we fight and die. Just by looking at my friends, I knew what they picked. Moss wanted to help, and knowing Rocket, he would follow Moss and me on whatever decision we made.

To clear my mind for a minute, I decided to peek behind the trees into the land of Union Beria, or at least the part we were in. I looked at something that could be considered a village with buildings made out of huge tree stumps, stone, and large acorns. The village looked peaceful. There isn't anything strange about it, especially being a different realm, other than the oddly sized and unknown plants and the fact of having acorn homes. Everything looked so perfect.

I was lost in my thoughts when Rocket came up from behind me. " I never knew acorns could grow *that* big."

I jumped at the sound of his voice, "Shit, dude! You scared the hell out of me," I turned, hitting his arm.

"Sorry," Rocket giggled as we looked back at the village.

I continued to watch, "Hey, Rocket? Can I ask you somethin'?"

Rocket laid his head peacefully on my shoulder, "Shoot." I averted my eyes away from the Russian boy's face, still watching the small village of people.

"What do you think we should do? I don't want to make a mistake," I worried. Rocket looked at me. I could never tell his emotions. He is like a blank canvas sometimes, and it can be hard to see how he feels.

"Well, I'm not sure. You know that what you choose, I will choose. Does that help with your question, Cherry?" Rocket smirked when he finished his sentence.

"I will slap you if you call me that again, but yes, it does," I roll my eyes. Am I that red in the face? Goddamnit, he always likes to point it out when it happens. I wish I weren't always so weird when he does this stuff. Normal guys don't react like this with their friends, right?

I continued to look at the people through the trees. There was one place I was drawn to in particular: an enormous stone house from the center of the village. I watched as someone came out of the stone house. They wore a long red and black ombre dress with various white patches. She had long, tight red curls in pigtails, which looked similar to Moss's hair when she didn't have her braids. Her skin was dark, but she had lighter spots that danced her skin. I believe those spots are vitiligo as they looked similar to it. The weirdest part was that they had a mushroom top on their head. Looking more at her, I saw she had pointy ears, too!

"Woah, guys, look at this person? Creature? I don't know what she is, but they're–" I started to say.

"Pretty! Now move over," Moss shuffled me over to look at the girl. She usually looked at women in awe, hearts for eyes, if I had to say.

How she looked at girls was like how I sometimes looked at Rocket. We looked at them with big, soft eyes and saw their gaze as if they were a Muse. I've always speculated that she didn't like guys much, and well, she doesn't. I've witnessed her kick a guy in the nuts after he called her a slur after she ignored his blatant harassment. I advise you not to harass a girl who is a brown belt in karate. Well, don't harass a girl in general. (Don't be a dumbass, guys.)

After a while, we made the decision. Rocket, Moss, and I walked up to Mourn to tell her.

"We have decided to stay. Now, we don't know what is in store for us here and if we will die or not. But if this world somehow blessed us and we are Pures, we want to help," I told the Goddess.

Mourn smiled, "Oh, thank you, children! You are forever in our debt for going out to help us. I will inform the others of your arrival so you can meet them. Give me one moment," Mourn got up, making her way out of the forest. She walked to the stone house as the mushroom girl Moss awed over came out again. They spoke briefly, and then we saw a hand making a come-here motion toward us. We followed as motioned to do. As we walked out of the woods, I could see everything about the village in clearer light. Many mushroom people were out and about, and they happened to be short beings. They must have been only four feet tall. They all looked at us as we walked to Mourn. Whispers were shared throughout the mushroom people as they stared at us with their black-button-like eyes. When we reached the house, Mourn told us to go inside with her. Entering through the door, Rocket, Moss, and I were motioned to a table with other people. I sat down, looking at all the others in front of me.

"Children, I would like to introduce you to the others and the village leaders," Mourn said.

"Hello. My name is Mrs. RedRoom. This is my wife, Mrs. Ink, and our daughter, Ruy RedInk. I am the leader of the Mushian people, also known as the Mushroom people. Welcome to [10]Ascomycota Island," Mrs. RedRoom said with an English-like accent.

I looked at Mrs. RedRoom and her wife, Mrs. Ink. RedRoom had a dark crimson afro that only reached a bit past her ears. She wore a beige cardigan with a red dress underneath and had a Fly Agaric mushroom on her head. Her skin was precisely like that of her daughter, the girl we saw in the forest moments before.

Then I looked over at Mrs. Ink. Her brown wavy hair was down and curled against her pale skin. She had a black and gray dress on, with the design of drips at the ends of it.

---

[10] **Ascomycota:** *(As·co·my·co·ta)*

She wore her Inkcap mushroom on her head and had black-thin framed glasses.

Mrs. RedRoom began to introduce the people that sat in front of us.

"These are some of the children from our colony. MariGold Poppy, a Floralin; Acorn Meg, a Gnomian; Clover Lockhilo, a Fairyian; Peep, the cutest little Trollian." She stopped behind each of their chairs with a smile. "And these two are Darwin Pakín, a Warlock, and Wasma Lovin, a Witch. I've known these two since they were very young, especially Wasma." The kids we faced all said hello to us themselves.

"Nice to meet you all. My name is Cricket Mont, and this is Rocket Chili and Moss Brine. And we are Pures, apparently," I told the group that sat before us.

Darwin, the Warlock who sat across from me, was a dark-skinned boy with black shoulder-length locs and brown eyes. He was wearing a white t-shirt with a red sweatshirt tied sideways over his chest and had blue jeans on. The emotions on his face were indecipherable, just like Rocket. From what Mourn told us, Humans harmed their home and its people. No wonder why he seems so emotionless around us.

Wasma, the girl beside Darwin, had long, dark blue wavy hair in a loose ponytail. She wore a sweater vest over a fishnet shirt and a long skirt that must have had every shade of blue and black in it. Wasma's eyes were a beautiful green, and she wore blue eyeshadow on her eyelids and red lipstick on her lips. Her ears were pointy like elf ears, and they moved with any slight movement of her face. Also, she had a belt around her waist that held colorful bottles and a knapsack. Wasma's arms were crossed, and her face looked like she didn't want to be there. Either she doesn't like us, or she just has a resting bitch face. Maybe it's a good idea to keep the joke that she must *really* like the color blue to myself if I want to live. She looks like the type of girl who can break my ribs if I joke like that. I did notice something small about her, though. She had these neck movements, which I believe are called tics. It was so quick that I don't think anyone would have realized she had them.

After the Witch, Wasma was the Fairyian Clover. Clover's hair was purple and in corn rows that ended in braids. Some of her hair was formed into two afro buns on both sides of her head, which made everything very symmetrical. Her ears have two points instead of the standard one-point elf ears. She had dark tan skin and two different colored eyes, one red and one yellow. Clover wore a navy blue cropped top, matching skort, and mismatched colored shoes. Her left shoe was yellow, and her right shoe was red, the exact opposite of her eyes. Over her chest hung a bow and an arrow case over her shoulder. The one thing that could be seen from anywhere on her was her translucent pink wings! Clover seemed to be the only one that was physically carefree. Her body language showed me that she was a happy person at heart.

On Clover's lap sat Peep. To be honest, I'm not entirely sure what it was. It looked like a mixture of moss, rock, and dirt, which I believe it is. Peep looked so fluffy, though, because of the moss. It even gave it the soft look of a blanket. It was something called a Trollian, which I would have never thought of as a moss and rock creature.

Next was Acorn, the short, ginger, curly-haired Gnomian boy. He has longer pointed ears, green eyes, and a face full of freckles. He wore an olive-green shirt, gray shorts, and a brown satchel that hung over his shoulder with an ax sticking out. His whole look and attitude gave me a Boy Scout vibe: very earthy and outdoorsy.

The last of the kids in front of us differed from the others. That was MariGold. She had orange heart-shaped flower petals in pigtails for hair, which ended in red tips, black eyes, and green skin but with a patch around her mouth that was a yellowish-brown color. Her arms were individual flower leaves, feet of roots, and ears with six points and small piercings. Even her eyelashes were the same type of petal as her hair! MariGold wore a gray and pink dress with a woven belt and a turquoise beaded necklace. MariGold seemed to have a kind spirit like Moss, with a delightful smile.

Mourn wasn't kidding about this place being magical. For crying out loud, I'm sitting in front of a group of people that could be considered fairy tales in our realm.

Mrs. RedRoom began to explain to us what was going on. "The colonies of Union Beria have been under attack recently by Humans. It started to show signs of worsening two months ago when the South Wing started deteriorating. Humans have been killing off the Tree Guardians, who protected the colonies from harm. When the Tree Guardians are killed, their magic leaves and anything they create dies with them."

"Now, children. Our creators need your help, and if we don't, we all will be in danger of deteriorating just like our home. If we can stop them from doing anything more and fight back, we have a chance to rebuild," Mrs. Ink spoke up after her wife with a similar accent.

"That explains the letters then. Are the Tree Guardians sure we can do this? We are just kids, well most of us are," Wasma replied.

"She makes a very valid point; we don't know what we're up against," Acorn adds to Wasma's words.

"That's why we had Mourn bring them," Mrs. RedRoom looked over at Rocket, Moss, and me.

"Wait, what? How are we supposed to help? Like Wasma said, we're kids, just like them," Moss objected.

"Well, we are Humans. Technically, shouldn't we have more insight into what they're like?" I clarified. "From what I know historically, they have dangerous weapons and powerful guns. They don't care who is in front of them; they'll shoot, and they will kill whoever gets in the way. These weapons can destroy almost anything, and they have. Cultures and generations of families, all gone because of war, colonization, and genocide."

Everyone stared at me while I talked. The atmosphere in the stone house was tense, and the air felt heavy. As I spoke, I started putting more things together in my head. The trucks rushing by the town, the newspaper theories, the earthquakes, and why Father got a call from his old superiors to come back; everything *would* make sense if it all is connected. It's hard to hear these people talk about the horrible things that we Humans have done to them both from history and what is happening in front of our eyes.

The conversation moved to Darwin, the Warlock, who took out the letter Wasma spoke of and read it to everyone in the room.

"To Whom It May Concern;

You may or may not know if you have received this letter that our colonies are in DANGER. Humans that were once nice and friendly have begun to kill us Guardians, one by one. We need your help. We have sent this message to one person from each colony. All members of your group shall meet on Ascomycota Island. You will meet your group: MariGold Poppy, Acorn Meg, Clover Lockhilo, Peep, Wasma Lovin, and Darwin Pakín. Hopefully, the others will be on their way with the River Guardian, Goddess Mourn, by then. These children are Keith Chili, Moss Brine, and Cricket Mont. Now, children of the colonies, don't be afraid of the others. They are Human, BUT they are Pures, making them children of the colonies as much as you are. There is a map, which was also given to you with this letter. This will help you get to The Center without Humans spotting any of you. The map will guide you through underground turns, unknown to most, that will eventually bring you to the Towers of Unity. Once you arrive, the One will find what is awaiting for Him. I know it may be dangerous, but our colony's future fate is in your hands. Save us from the Humans. We don't have much time left till everything is gone. Just remember, IF WE DIE, YOU ALL WILL TOO. It is scary but true. Now, good luck on your travels, and please stay safe.

Sincerely,
The Elder Tree Guardians"

Silence hit everyone. That was definitely a way to write that letter. These Tree Beings put all the pressure on eight kids and one troll to save their world all in one letter.

I began to fidget my hand under the table until Rocket grabbed it with his own. He always had a way to calm people down, even without words.

Mourn approached me and my friends, "I must leave you to your adventures. When everything is done, and over, you will return home. Remember, children, you have the power of this world within you, and you will find out more about it while on your journey. Please be safe. I believe in you with all of my heart. Moss, Rocket, Cricket, I hope to see you again." She put her hand to my face and smiled, then exited the house after bowing her head to Mrs. RedRoom and Mrs. Ink.

Chapter 5
As We Begin

"Ruy dear, I have some business to take up with. May you be helpful to our guests?" Mrs. RedRoom asked her child.

"Of course, Mum. I will take them to the village meeting building. Follow me, please." Ruy turned to us, opened the front door, and escorted us to the building.

Like before, many Mushian people were working outside. I noticed that all the Mushian-folk were women, or at least non-male. I remember learning about mushrooms, including Ascomycota, in biology class in ninth grade. They are known to produce asexually, which confused me when I saw the Mushian people. I eventually asked Ruy about it while we walked to the building she was bringing us to. She explained to me that all Mushians are female or sexless beings and that when the creatures were first created, they used the budding method to produce offspring. However, that ended up with the children looking the same as their mother, which was less than ideal. Eventually, after years of tests and failed attempts, they created a way to combine the DNA of two Mushians and produce offspring asexually. I was very shocked when I heard about such things. It is amazing how intelligent these beings are, even when separated from all parts of the colonies on off-land islands.

All nine of us sat on the benches lined in rows in the meeting building as Ruy stood in the front of the room. The Mushian took the map from Darwin and quickly drew out what the map contents showed on the back wall.

"Alright, now this is your map. We are here," she makes an 'x' on the wall, "and this is the tunnel that goes to The Center. It looks like there are a couple of turns and forks within them, but if you go straight from here, make a right here, a left there, and then go through the middle one here, you should make it to The Center within a day or so! After walking, I think you should rest somewhere for the night. There is a place called the TreeTrunk Motel that isn't too far from the tunnel exit. Here is the Treen name for it." The wall was covered in lines and X's, which made it hard to look at. Ruy spells out the motel's name on the right side of the map, but it wasn't in any language I've ever seen before. It was all symbols. They referred to it as *Treen*, which I'd never heard of before. My eyes trace over each symbol twice, looking at the intricate details in each letter.

Rocket had to have read my mind because he raised his hand and asked, "Um, what 'tis Treen? I don't think I've ever seen it before." His thick accent makes his words slur again.

"Oh!" Clover's ears perked up, "Treen is the language of the Tree Guardians and the Trollians. It's more of a written language for most people, but Trolls and the Elders still speak it. Us Fairyians can understand Treen to a point as well. The language is taught to the children of the North Wing, where we fairies live when we are young. Some of it sticks, some of it doesn't. It is common for fairies to understand Treen when spoken, not so much written, though it varies from Fairyian to Fairyian. It is scarce for anyone that isn't a Fairyian to comprehend Treen, written or heard, but there are always the few that do." Once Clover finished explaining, Rocket nodded, confirming that he understood what she said.

"Now that we have everything covered on how to get to The Center, I would like to give you all Golden Quins for when you go to the motel for a room. Quins and Quiks are the currencies of the colonies. This can also help with trading if you get the chance. Each pouch has twenty-five Quins, and a normal room should cost about seventy-eight Quiks. Please do use them responsibility," Ruy gives all nine of us a heavy but small bag of coins.

"Thank you so much. We will use these only when needed," Moss thanked her.

After discussing the plan to get to The Center, Ruy left to speak with their mums for a moment. This gave us time to talk with each other.

"So, you are Pures. I've heard many things about Pures in books from the libraries in the East Wing. Do you guys know what powers you have?" Acorn, the Gnomian asked us.

"Not really. All we know is that the symbols Mourn gave us are supposed to relate to our power somehow," I said.

"What kind of marks do you have? Maybe we can help you figure it out?" MariGold replied.

"Well, mine is a sunflower," Moss says.

"Mine is of a raven," Rocket said after Moss.

"And mine is... a cricket," I roll my eyes.

"Ah, that is ironic," Wasma chuckled. The others grouped around the three of us to look at our palms.

"What's ironic?" I questioned.

"The marks are literally from you. Moss, your sweater is covered in sunflowers. Rocket, your jacket has what I think is a raven on it. And Cricket, well—it's your name. It explains why you have those specific ones," Wasma points out.

"If your symbols are related to your powers, then... Moss, you probably have something to do with flowers. Rocket, you probably have something to deal with intelligence or transformation," Acorn thinks. "When coming to Cricket's... I'm not sure. A cricket is blind and doesn't have much to it. They are only good at being everywhere and annoying-" He stopped mid-sentence, "I don't mean that for you, though." I hear the guilt in his voice.

"It's alright, I don't take offense to it," I gave a weak smile, trying to reassure Acorn that it was alright, though my voice was flat as paper while I spoke.

Rocket looked over at me. He knew I was lying. My face was probably contorting with emotions. Were my eyebrows lifted? My face scrunched up? I just didn't want to make Acorn feel bad for saying something he didn't know would hit me close to home. I've always hated the name Cricket, but when I was growing up, I loved it. It was unique like me, but Mama said something that made me rethink everything I thought about my name and myself.

*****

"You are so fucking annoying, Cricket. Didn't Mommy just say she had a hangover? Ugh! No wonder why we named you such a ridiculous name. You're just as insufferable as the real thing. I really regret not taking that pill sometimes," Catherine's words spilled into my mind. I knew I wasn't that stupid not to notice that she always hated me, let alone regretted me.

*****

I was six years old when she said that to me. We still lived in Queens then, so she would have to come to my school to pick me up and then catch the train to return home. Mama usually had the time to pick me up as Father worked late most days. Mama and I were waiting on the subway platform. We were late to the subway that day and had to wait for the next one to come by. I was telling my mom about my day like normal. At that time, I didn't realize she had a hangover from the previous night. However, I was talking without realizing her problem, and it made her angry with me. I started questioning if she even liked me after that day. I was her kid. Why wouldn't she like me? For the next couple of years, I suffered with her coming with me to the subway until 1977. That was the year Father, and I moved to LongEdge after the custody battle. I still never told Father about that day. I don't think I will ever be able to.

Moss and Rocket shook my shoulders as if in a panic. I must have zoned out for a while not to know what was happening. My eyes refocus, trying to blink away the blurry tears, as my friends grabbed my arms and quickly got me off the bench. Ruy came back into the meeting building, rushing to lock the doors.

"Everyone! Over here!" Ruy, with panic in her voice, ran over to us. She stopped at a large bench near the front of the room. "I need help moving this!"

We all came over to her to help push the heavy bench out of the way. Ruy began scrubbing off her map drawing from the wall as we did that.

"What is going on?!" Clover asked.

"Humans! They must have found out you were here somehow. Did any of you make a disturbance when you left?" Ruy questioned the group while she finished scrubbing.

Darwin and Wasma looked at each other with worry. "We probably set off the guards when we escaped the Hell Wing," Wasma replied. I assume she was speaking about the South Wing.

"My Guardian- it doesn't matter now, you must leave for The Center," the Mushian spoke.

Once we moved the bench, we discovered a hole in the floor, *the tunnel entrance.* Our heads turned as we heard the yells from the Mushian people from outside. "Go! I promised my mums that you would make it there safely. You must leave now. Please be safe on your travels," Ruy looked at all of us with worry.

"What about you and your people? What will happen to you?" Darwin questioned.

"We will take care of ourselves. We might be small, but we will fight. Our home is in your hands. Now go, please!" She yelled back. She then started to push us into the tunnel one by one.

After all of us were stuffed inside the tunnel, the bench was pushed back over the entrance, leaving us in total darkness. We waited for what felt like forever to hear something from the other side in the silent hole.

"We should start moving. The tunnels should get larger once we are away from the surface. For now, we crawl," Wasma told us. She took one of her bottles out from her belt and shook it. Once she did that, it began to glow a bright yellow. Now, having a light, we started crawling into the secret underground tunnels with Wasma in the front.

It only took fifty minutes of crawling until the tunnel got larger. There was a step down from the narrow tunnel into a larger one where we could stand. When we entered this part, a blue light flooded our sight. At least in this part, the tunnels were made of transparent material, as if a tube. This made it easy for us to see the tunnel's location. It just happened to be in the deep water.

"Holy shit- Are we underwater?" Rocket's eyes wandered.

"I guess so. Is there something wrong with that?" Darwin asked him.

"I've never been a huge fan of deep water. I'll be okay, though. Hopefully," Rocket looked at Darwin with an uncertain expression.

My eyes could not stop from wandering through the water around us. It was beautiful to me, even if Rocket was shaken by it. The animals seemed so unbothered by our presence. Soon enough, the anxious tension in the tunnel grew calmer than from how we entered. Darwin and I walked behind the others as they made conversation. Moss was talking to MariGold and Clover. All I heard from them were tiny giggles that glued itself to the sides of the tube tunnel. I could tell they hit it off just by the smiles I saw on their faces. Rocket and Wasma talked to each other about who knows what while Acorn and Peep strolled together. The Gnomian boy was just talking to the Trollian about random things that popped into his head, and the Troll peeped in response. I assume that's what Clover meant by Treen being spoken, at least when it comes to Trolls. To everyone else, all we hear are peeps, even though they are talking just like us. It makes sense why they call it Peep.

"Darwin, what is it like being a Warlock? That's what you call yourself, right? I hope you don't mind me asking. " I asked the boy next to me.

"Oh, it's alright. I have pretty interesting powers, but I never really used them growing up. Sometimes it sucks. You know, being a Warlock in the South Wing nowadays," Darwin replied.

"How come?" My head tilted.

"Well, I have the same type of magic as Wasma. Although, I just have a couple more broken bells and damaged whistles. But my home was taken over by Humans so they could make us use a form of dark magic forbidden in Union Beria. Then there are the nightmares and recurring visions. All that jazz," he said. Like I said before, his face is hard to read.

"Right, you're from the South Wing. Mourn told us a bit about it. I'm incredibly sorry about us Humans. Our kind has been trying to conquer places for hundreds, maybe even thousands of years," I apologized.

"I believe there are Humans who are better than these pricks. I'd like to say that you guys are an example of that, as well as me," Darwin replied.

"What do you mean by that?" I asked.

"My father was a Human. It isn't the first time Humans have ever come to Union Beria, and it definitely won't be the last. My mom told me that my dad was a geographer back in India and that in his free time, he studied ruins. While researching, he stumbled into one of the portals and came here. He then met my mom and had me. Then, one day, he left to go back to your realm. Seventeen years later, I am taking care of my mother by myself, forced to work for Humans, and here we are now." He explains.

"I'm sorry to hear that happened. But I guess that makes you similar to us? Part

Human, part magical being," I tried to make the conversation less sad.

A slight smirk came from Darwin's lips, "Yeah, I guess it does."

He looks over to where Wasma is. She was still speaking with Rocket and now Clover.

"How did you guys meet?" I realized who he was looking at.

"Wasma and I? I've known her since I was eight. She was a year older than me, but it didn't stop us from clicking. We met at one of those play parks in those big, colorful plastic hangouts that always made you think you were in a castle. Since that day, we have been inseparable. Our family lives are what made us connect at first. Her dad was a jerk, and her mom committed suicide due to terrible postpartum depression after she was born. My dad left me, and my mom is ill. So, we understood each other to a point. It's ironic now thinking about it. That day, we were both hiding from our parents, of course, for different reasons," Darwin sighed, then shifted his shoulders. If I knew anything from reading body language, it was his way of turning the conversation to a different light. "And I've always... you know, liked her, though I think she has someone else on her mind," Darwin's eyes wandered to Wasma, who had a tint of pink on her face while talking to Clover. "Anyway, how about you? When did you meet the sunflower girl and raven boy?"

We laughed at the names he called my friends. "Oh? Well, I can understand why you like her. She is pretty. Personally, I'm not into the gals." I wish I could have shut my mouth before I spoke, but it was too late. I made an awkward smile, looking at him and then at Rocket.

"Oh! You- you like him, don't you?" He smiled at me, speaking in a whisper.

I looked at him, a bit surprised. He didn't care? I've always been pretty open about my sexuality at home with my dad and with my friends, but I don't usually go around telling people that I'm queer. Why didn't I feel the normal way I do when I bring that up? Usually, I'd try to take cover just in case the person got angry or repulsed by me. Union Beria has me acting the opposite of myself.

"Is it obvious?" My face felt hot with embarrassment.

"Kinda, but it will be our little secret for both of us," Darwin said, pointing his pinky at me. From that moment forward, we pinky swore our promise to each other to keep our secret crushes on our best friends to ourselves. "Anyway, you don't have to be embarrassed for telling me. It's not the end of the world if you like him."

I continued to smile at him. He had no clue that it was like the end of the world back home if you were gay. But I didn't want to tell him that, so I smiled and nodded.

I brought us back to our conversation from before. I explained to the Warlock how I met Rocket and Moss in school. It felt easy to talk to him. We continued to make small talk, one thing after the next. He spoke about what the Wings in Union Beria were like, and I told him about what it was like living in Queens and LongEdge. Even though I only met this boy barely two hours ago, I was telling him things that I'd tell my best friends. That's when Darwin asked about my family.

"How about your family? What are they like?" He asked politely.

My eyes refused to make eye contact with him. "I live with my father in LongEdge. My mother, Catherine, lives in Queens. They divorced in '77, and Father and I moved to Ohio the same year. My father is an amazing dad, but Catherine, she's a cold-hearted bitch," I said.

"Damn, is she *that* bad,"

"Yeah, she is. Although, I can give her some credit. She's been drug-free for the past few years, and I am happy she kicked heroin. But all I know is she is still a drunk and has basically forgotten she already had a son. She is getting remarried and caring for two new step-kids like I don't exist. I haven't seen her in person for almost eight years, and she barely calls. Now, she *dares* to come into my life and say she is taking me away from my father for the rest of the summer. Catherine wants me to get all buddy-buddy with a man I don't know and two kids who probably never knew she had a son. I can't even fathom why she wants to be in my life again. She failed at being my mother the first time, and I don't think I owe her another chance," I ranted.

"My Gods- your mother sounds horrible," he paused, "Does your dad know you're here?"

"No, he doesn't." The feeling of guilt made itself clear on my tongue.

"He's probably worried sick about you," the boy mentioned.

"All of our parents are probably worried..." I began to say, "I got into a fight with him the night before I ran away. I was upset. I wasn't thinking, and now I'm here and going to fight alongside people and creatures I have only seen in fairytales. There is no turning back from here, is there?" My eyes shot to Darwin's.

"Absolutely not, but I promise you that we will all get home to your families safely— each and every one of us," Darwin said, placing a hand on my shoulder and giving me a small smile.

Moss had turned to Darwin and me a bit after our main conversation. She grabbed both of our hands and pulled us towards the group. When we joined them, I realized they were talking about themselves, just like what Darwin and I were doing. It was safe to assume that only a few of us here knew much about the others.

Wasma wasn't the biggest fan of the idea, but MariGold said that if we were going to walk for hours, we should do something to fill up our time. The Witch didn't want to argue her logic, so she agreed.

"I've lived in the East Wing's orphanage since I was five. Honestly, it is a lovely place. All of the Floralin women imams are like mothers to me and practically made me who I am today. While living in the orphanage, I met my now girlfriend, Lilly Petaldrop. My life before I met her was depressing. I struggled with who I was; she helped me feel like me. I used to go by Gold, but now I am MariGold. I wanted to keep that name with me, as I'm still the same being, just now a girl," MariGold told us with a tender grin that could brighten a room and, in our case, a tube.

I looked over at Moss. A huge smile grew on her face while she listened. She grabbed MariGold's 'hand' (as her arms were one big leaf), "We are truly the same then." MariGold hugged Moss, not breaking the beam on her face.

Everyone had their chance to speak. Moss told her story about what it was like to grow up in the wrong body, knowing that for years but not being able to put a word to it. "The day I saw the protests and the faces of women like me, holding signs and fighting to be seen, I knew who and what I was. I was Moss, a *transgender woman*." As she spoke, her arm was linked with MariGold's leaf arm. It was as if they were comforting each other and saying, 'I see you.'

Wasma talked about her mom and Julius, her abusive father. She mentioned that she had wanted to be a doctor since she was young. In her own words, she said, "I want to help the women that need the support my mother wasn't given when she had me. I want to save lives." Wasma spoke with the most emotion I've seen come from her. Once she finished speaking, she quickly wiped tears from her eyes, and her face returned to showing little emotion.

Acorn told us about what it was like raising himself from a young age. He had seven brothers and six sisters and was in the middle of all of them. Acorn got a bit teary-eyed when explaining how forgotten he felt being in such a big family. "I had to grow up without a family to lean on. I was lucky to find someone who helped care for me when my family couldn't, my Uncle Jolin. Man, I miss him so much." Even though he had a careless family, he still had someone who ensured he was fed, clothed, and loved.

After Acorn, Rocket spoke. Though having heard the stories about his family in Russia millions of times and his difficulty learning English and having to teach his parents the language, Moss and I listened to each word he said. His words felt like honey by the way he talked without one stutter.

Darwin was next, saying the same things he told me about. How he lives with his sick mother and that his dad left him. But Darwin mentioned something new— why he hates using his powers. "I was cursed with a prophecy that I will one day live out. I wish I hadn't listened to my mother's words when she told me. My powers keep me up at night." From what he said, one of the perks of a Witch is making and receiving prophecies for people. As his mother was a Witch, her job was to notify someone if she received a prophecy about them. He refused to talk about his powers and the prophecy in further detail.

We sat in silence for a moment before Clover began talking. She told us about her two sisters, Ember and Angel, and her mom and dad. How she cried herself to sleep the night in which she received two letters in the mail. One of the letters was from the Elder Tree Guardians, and the other was from the delivery department where her father worked. For months, she helped care for her baby sisters while her father was out doing flight deliveries by force from the Humans. That night, she was told that Humans killed her dad, and now she had to go out and fight them. "I didn't want to leave my family after my dad was taken forever from us. I didn't want to turn up like him, *dead*. Before I left, I gave my sisters hugs and kisses and even gave my mom a book with my goodbyes written just in case."

I could tell she didn't want the spotlight on her anymore, or she would bawl. She wiped her face of tears and then went on to help translate a bit for Peep. Its peeps filled the tube tunnel to the brim. According to the translation, Peep has many siblings, all born in Union Beria's grounds. It has been alive for over a hundred years and has seen generations of creatures come and go. Peep mentioned that its family members were created when the colonies were first made, saying that the magic from the Tree Guardians went into the grounds and started making the Trollians from there. Then, when trying to find a home, they came across caves in the depths of the North Wing. So, the Trollians migrated from the West Wing to the North, set up camp, and made the caves their homes for future generations.

Finally, it was my turn. I started by mentioning Father and Cathrine and when Father and I left our home from Queens for good, though I did not explain why we did. I told them some of the things I said to Darwin, and their faces became sad again. It's not like any of us had a good life at home. Why did it matter when it was me? Why are they sad now that a Human/Pure was saying it?

I tried to glance over it and focus on another thought. That's when I heard something. This *something* came from outside the tube. I stopped walking for a moment, turning my head.

"Are you alright?" Clover called out.

I shifted my eyes over to her direction to look at her. She wasn't even talking to me; Clover was talking to Acorn. I heard it again. Then I got wind of Wasma talking to Darwin.

"Dar?" Wasma began to panic and curse under her breath. From the corner of my eye, I watched her scrutinize through the knapsack on her belt. The sound was getting louder. It was the sound of *singing.*

"What is going on? You can't hear that song?" Rocket looked over at Moss.

She shrugs at him, "No, I don't. What's going on?"

"It's a Siren. Take these boys; it will block out her song," Wasma said. She handed Darwin, Acorn, Rocket, and me earplugs, and we followed her instructions.

After we did, something hit the side of the tube. We turned to the bang, but nothing was there except the dark sea. Then it happened again, and we saw a tale disappear in the deep water underneath.

"I can't see anything in this abyss. Why is a Siren here?" Darwin asked.

"We must be trespassing through their cove," Acorn replied. As soon as he spoke, another bang was made.

When turning to it, we saw the Siren. Her movements were smooth and delicate as she swam around the tube. The Siren's skin was scaly and a gray shade that melted into a navy-blue tale. Her pitch-black hair came down long past her waist. Over her bare breasts was a top of gold chains and pearls that stretched to her upper arms. Jewels, all kinds of gold and pearl, swam delicately around her neck, waist, arms, and tail.

"She's breathtaking," Moss said.

"That's the point. Sirens use their song and gaze to seduce and attract men and sailors. Then, when the men come, the Siren drowns them or even causes their boats to crash, ultimately bringing them to their deaths," Acorn explains.

"I've heard about them before. In our realm, there are folktales and myths about Sirens and many other creatures like them," Moss replied.

I looked down at where Peep was. It was trying to use its rock paws to claw at the Siren. I'm not going to lie; it was an adorable sight you could only see once in your life. When I looked back up, the Siren was snarling at us, making my skin crawl.

"Holy-" I jumped when I saw her.

She banged more on the tube. The Siren wanted to get to us. Her mouth opened, and even with the earplugs in, I could hear the scream she let out. The tunnel started to shake, making us need to grab the side of it so we didn't fall. It felt like I was in a Magic 8 ball being asked a question.

"Lady, we aren't here to harm you!" Darwin yelled out.

"Can she even hear us if we say something?" Clover asked.

"Yes, Sirens have wonderful hearing, but she is one stubborn Siren," Acorn acknowledged.

The Siren glared at Acorn, "What are you here for?! You are in the Siren Cove." Her voice was strong, as was her accent. It sounded similar to how Australian people sound, but her voice range was airy, which is odd as she is speaking through water.

"Siren, miss! We promise you no harm. All we are trying to do is get to The Center to save all creatures that live here. You know of the war going on?" MariGold called out.

The Siren's eyes widened, and she swam to the other side of the tube as if looking us over.

"I see... my apologies, travelers," she spoke through her teeth, "I hate the male presence of some of you. How would I know if you were good?"

"I can understand to a point. You have no reason to trust us. May I ask what your name is, Siren? It is the least you can give us after trying to put us under your hypnosis and, well, kill us," Darwin stood firm.

"You have a point," she cleared her throat, "My name is Cyrus Monroe. You are looking at the first *and* only Ancient Siren breed of Union Beria!"

"Ancient Siren?" I wondered.

"There are two types of Sirens out here: the fish version and the bird version. I just happen to be a hybrid. I look like this in the cove, but on land, I am a beautiful being with rich black wings and talons that could rip a male's heart out! As you can tell, someone like me is born one in a thousand years. All my fellow Sirens are just fish, and those birds aren't that fun to be around," Cyrus spoke with cockiness.

"Woah! Wait, aren't you the one that killed those Humans by the North Wing earlier this week?" Clover asked with a hint of excitement in her voice.

"Yes, I am. Good to know that my stories get told around," Cyrus said with a sharp smirk, her shark-like teeth showing. A swift change of emotions appeared on her face. "My eyes are up here, boys," her smile dropped, snarling down at us again. I turned my head to look at Rocket. Of course, he was staring.

"Oh, sorry!" he smiled awkwardly. That smile always made me pink just looking at him. He looks so pretty.

"Well, Cyrus, it's nice to meet you," MariGold said, trying not to show her worries, which were evident to my ears.

A noise came from the ground of the tube tunnel. Peep began peeping loudly with some growls in between them.

"Peep peep peep peep. Peep peep peep peep peep," the Trollian said.

"Clover, translation, please?" Wasma asked the Fairyian.

"Oh, right! Peep asked if there was anything more you wanted to tell us so we could leave. It isn't very fond of a Sirens' presence," Clover translates.

"Well... rude, but yes. If what you tell me is true about going to The Center to help the colonies, you should know that Humans have boats out in the water. From the description, it seems you are the ones the evil men talk about." Cyrus herself even had a bit of worry on her face.

"Oh." I gulped.

"We should get moving then. Thank you for your warning, Cyrus," Wasma thanks the Siren.

Cyrus nodded, "Of course. I hope to see you all soon, and from how everything looks now, I will most likely will. Well, either as fish food or saviors. Whatever form, I'm just a siren call away." She wiped her tail at us, evilly laughing as she swam away.

"That was nice of her for the warning," Moss shrugged.

"I guess you can call that nice. She was trying to lure our boys to their deaths *and* called us fish food," Wasma replied.

"Eh, I'll let this one slide because she was giving us a warning," I joked.

From there, we started our long journey again. It was going to be a long day and a very long night.

Chapter 6
The Center

*M*inutes feel like hours, and hours feel like days. The tube tunnels felt like they would never end when we wished they did. We even hit an area within the tube that had water spewing into it. There was a crack in the wall, letting water in. Thankfully, Acorn had something to patch the crack, so no more water came into the tube. However, that still meant we had to walk through a foot of water. Clover even had to hold Peep so it didn't get wet.

The journey started to feel like it was coming to an end when the water around the tunnel became clearer, and I could start to see the sea floor.

"We only have maybe a hundred feet until we hit the surface. We might need to crawl soon, so get ready to be uncomfortable again," Wasma told the group as we all groaned.

My eyes started to feel tired, but thankfully, we were going to this motel that

Ruy had told us about. By accident, I began to drift my body to where Rocket was.

"Are you alright? You look like you're about to fall over," Rocket said calmly.

"I'm just tired. None of us got to sleep before we left. Maybe you did on your flight home, but still," I replied, yawning.

"Ah, true. I slept most of the way home on the flight, so I got lots of energy!" He smiled at me. Just looking at him smiling is like seeing the sunrise early in the morning. It is like he is glowing from the inside out.

I must have been staring at him because Rocket gave me a smirk. "What?" I asked defensively.

"Nothing," he replied, looking forward now, still smirking. I wonder what that's about.

An hour or two had passed when we saw an orange light a little distance away. My knees hurt from crawling in the now narrow tunnel once again. A sigh of relief came over us when the light grew closer, but that's when Peep started to growl.

"Wait a moment. I think Peep senses something," Clover stated. We stopped as Peep smelled the air and bolted out of the tunnel. "PEEP, WAIT!" Clover yelled at it.

Trying to crawl fast was challenging and weird. Wasma peered her head out of the tunnel's entrance and quickly pulled herself back in.

"Crap..." Wasma whispered, "Everyone, stay as quiet as you can."

I could only guess what she saw from her pale expression: *Humans*. However, this still didn't explain why her face had lost all color. What did she see?

Moments later, we heard yelling, which caused us to climb out of the tunnel quickly. Now I understand why Wasma looked so sickly. Peep was attacking two Human soldiers. Its body had grown almost to the size of a tall child. The Trollian's claws sliced at the men's chests and bit their arms. This whole sight was an actual bloodbath. In seconds, the Humans fell to the ground, limp. I don't know how to describe this in any words. Although, I can say it reminded me much of *The Texas Chain-Saw Massacre*.

"Peep! What the hell! What if someone sees them like this? We would be dead meat!" Clover yelled at Peep.

"Peep peep."

"Saying sorry won't make two men return from the dead, Peep!" She continued to lecture the Trollian while Darwin walked over to the bodies.

His face looked puzzled as his eyes traced over the soldiers. "We should move them just in case there are more out here. Who wants to help me move these guys?" Darwin looked up.

Clover, Moss, and MariGold raised their arms, saying no, while Acorn shook his head.

"Yeah, hell no, dude," Moss replied.

"Waszy? Cricket? Rocket? Help a guy out?" He asked.

"Fine. I'm only doing this because this wouldn't be the first time I've had to," Wasma said.

"You've moved dead people before?" Rocket's eyes widened.

"None of you have seen what the South Wing is like, and that statement says that," her ponytail swung behind her as she walked over to Darwin.

I looked at Rocket with a shocked face. All he replied with was a shrug, then followed them.

Rocket and Wasma grabbed one of the men, and Darwin and I grabbed the other. Finding an empty cave and throwing them inside didn't take much effort. The only effort put into it was lifting the bodies themselves. When we returned from the cave, the sun started to set. Acorn passed a canteen of water to the four of us so we could wash any blood that had gotten on our skin.

"I think the motel Ruy told us about isn't that far away from here. Let's get a room and get some rest. If we are going to have to deal with any more of this stuff, I'm going to need some sleep at least," Darwin told the group. His fingers squeezed the bridge of his nose in frustration. We made our way quickly out of the forest, following Darwin as he guided us. Who knows if there are any more of those soldiers out here? It would be weird to stay at the crime scene made of your own accord.

Arriving at the TreeTrunk Motel within less than an hour, I could understand the name more clearly. It was a huge log of wood that was sideways on the ground. We entered the motel and were greeted by a man at the front desk. He gave us two keys, and we paid for two connecting rooms, which we used most of our Quins to purchase. Upon finding the rooms, the girls and us guys separated. The girls, Clover, MariGold, Moss, and Wasma, entered room 46B. And us boys, Acorn, Rocket, Darwin, Peep, and I entered room 47B.

We settled in quickly. Peep curled up on the floor, and the four of us shared the two beds. Darwin and Acorn took the bed near the door, and Rocket and I took the other near the closed window. My body had been exhausted from being on my feet all day long. As my head hit the pillow, a thought slipped into my mind. *I hope Father is doing alright.* That's when I fell into a deep, profound sleep.

Chapter 7
Run Fast For
Your Father

*D*reaming is supposed to be fun and light. Somewhere, you can drift off to when everything else is scary and dark; when they are, those are nightmares. But sometimes there is an in-between. At least there is for me. It's not fun and light, but neither scary nor dark. Well, maybe it's always dark. I call it the void when you can't dream of anything good or bad. It's just darkness. Usually, that is when I sleep the best. There's no worry about waking up in a cold sweat or waking up from a good dream you know you won't be able to return to. Nevertheless, I wish I dreamt of something. I would have taken a nightmare over the void this time. It felt so lonely, so cold, and too dark for my liking. Typically, I enjoy the darkness of the void I look through, but something feels off. I've never felt this way while in this state of mind before. Though there was nothing,

I could feel something without seeing it. Darkness worked in mysterious ways; I can tell you that.

I arose quickly with sweat dripping down my face. I didn't need a nightmare to make me jump out of bed. My feet dangled from the bedside as I sat there with my hands over my face. I could feel my pulse through my whole body, which felt strange. Trying not to freak out, the hairs on my neck rose. My back straightened as if a cold breeze had passed by. I turned slowly to see the door connecting the girl's room to ours. The doorknob was shaking vigorously. I got up quietly and cautiously unlocked the door. On the other side stood a very panicked, horribly shaken Moss.

"Moss, what's wrong? Did something happen?" I asked her, trying to grab her hands, but she pulled them away before I could do so.

"I-I had this nightmare... and I woke up to see this..." Her voice cracked as she spoke. Moss motioned me to look inside the girls' room. When I did, I saw why she looked so scared. The bed she slept on was bursting at the seams with sunflowers. There was even an imprint of where Moss had laid.

"Jesus, Moss. I don't know what to make of this," I told her honestly.

"It gets worse. The flowers were trying to wrap around me. One even wrapped around my neck, and the stem broke when I ripped it off, and I felt it. I felt the pain." Her eyes were full of tears. "Then there was the nightmare. You guys were laying in a field with these fucking sunflowers growing out of your mouths. You weren't responding when I tried to shake you guys awake. I was so scared."

I looked at Moss, now bawling her eyes out as we whispered to each other. I pulled her into a hug while she sobbed on my shoulder. Her knees gave way, and we both fell to the floor.

"I couldn't help any of you," Moss' voice was muffled.

"It was just an awful and terrible dream. I'm right here, Moss. I'm right here, and we are all alive," I tried soothing her. It took a bit for Moss to stop crying, but I gave her every second of my time.

It was still dark outside, so it was hard to tell what time it was. Moss walked over to the window as I examined the bed of sunflowers.

"Do you think it's those powers Mourn told us we had?" Moss asked, still looking out the window with little to no emotion.

"Maybe. It would make sense," I replied, looking back at her.

She nodded her head, not making eye contact. I could tell she was still spooked, and rightfully so. The poor thing was almost choked by her own sunflowers. I can still see the red mark around her neck.

I noticed a change in her eyes as she continued to look through the window. "Crick... do you see that over there?" Moss was pointing at something.

I walked over to her to see what she was talking about. I could see exactly what she saw when I peered from behind the curtains— Humans with flashlights near the motel.

"That's not good," I murmured.

"What should we do?" Asked Moss.

"Wake up the others, I guess. It would be risky to stay here. You go wake the girls, and I'll wake the guys." I mentioned to the girl next to me. Moss agreed and quickly hurried to wake the others.

I gently shook Darwin and Acorn awake. "Guys, wake up. We have company, and it's not the good kind."

It didn't take them long to jump out of bed and get their things together. I went over to Rocket and tried to shake him awake, but slightly less gentle. He didn't wake up, so I shook him harder. I knew he was a deep sleeper, but this felt like too much. When he still didn't wake up, I threw the covers off of him, and what I saw was both breathtaking and freaky. Under the covers lay Rocket and a massive set of shiny black wings caressed against the side of his body.

"Holy shit!" I couldn't control myself from speaking loudly.

Surprisingly, that's what woke Rocket up from his deep slumber. "What 'tis it?" The wings moved with him when he jumped up. He looked at me with confusion in his eyes. All I could do was point at his wings with my mouth dropped open. Rocket turned his head to see what I was pointing at. Instantly, he cursed out in Russian at the sight of the wings. I couldn't tell you if it was out of terror or excitement. I can't even understand what he said. All I could figure out was him saying the f-word a lot.

"Woah there. When the hell did you get wings?" Darwin looked over at Rocket now that he was entirely out of bed.

"I don't know! How do I make them go away?!" His face was much paler than average. I figured it out now; he was terrified.

"Rocket, we will figure that out later, but we need to get out of here," I tried to explain.

"Why? What happened?" He asked.

"Humans are near, and we need to leave now," I replied.

The girls entered our room. Wasma chuckled to herself at what she saw. "I see you found your power, Rocket," Wasma said. She walked over to him and put her hand over the wings. "They are so beautiful."

"Ah! Careful, they are sensitive!" Rocket swatted Wasma's hand away.

"I've never seen anything like this." Acorn mentioned, "Have you guys gotten your powers yet?" He looked over at Moss and me.

"Yeah, I got mine," Moss replied softly, probably remembering the sunflowers layering her bed.

"We could tell. Your bed was ripping from its seams with sunflowers," MariGold replied.

"Let's not talk about it," Moss said as I watched her look at the floor. Fear is still prominent in her eyes and voice.

"What about you, Cricket?" Clover asked me.

"I don't think I've gotten mine yet. Should I be worried?" I hesitantly spoke.

"Hey, everyone takes their own time when coming one with their power. Trust me," Darwin put his hand on my shoulder.

"Now, we should get out of here before the Humans spot us."

"You're right. They are way too close for comfort. All we need is one person to come to the motel, and we will get caught," Wasma declared.

"Alright! How do you think we should get out, though? We could take an alternate route until they clear away," Clover suggested.

"Maybe we should go through the Bewitched Forest. It will take us longer to get to the Towers of Unity, but it's a fair shot we can take. The thing is, we'd have to run past the Humans to enter. I think we'll lose them, though. The forest is thick enough that they will lose sight of us," Acorn explained.

"That's a good idea, Acorn. We'd have a good chance to get away from them if the forest is as thick as you say it is," Moss said, her confidence slowly returning.

"Wait, if we decide to go with this plan, there is also a chance that we could get lost and lose sight of each other," Acorn continued.

"I'll take the odds of those chances. If we get lost, we are bound to find each other at some point," Rocket uttered, patting Acorn's back with a smile.

All of us agreed to the plan. Clover would go first, with Peep in her arms, flying over the forest without the Humans seeing her. The rest of us would have to sneak out and run like we had never run before.

And that's precisely what we did. I watched as Clover and Peep flew away and disappeared into the forest's thick trees. Then, it was our turn.

We waited for the men to move some distance before we began running. My legs pumped against the ground, and my lungs filled with hot air. I've always hated running, and this reminded me of that. At some point, though, the Humans spotted us and began to chase us like hunting dogs.

The forest felt like it was closing in around me as the trees got thicker, and I started losing sight of the others. One by one, they left my view. After running a far distance, I hid behind a large tree. Even through the darkness, I knew something was on my trail. I could hear what was supposed to be the faint breathing and footsteps of someone following me against the silence of the woods around me, but it wasn't faint at all. Every crunch and every snap of leaves and twigs from the forest floor felt like it was screaming in my ears. Have you ever, on accident, turned the radio on in the car, and it was blasting music, and you instantly covered your ears? It felt like that, but I couldn't cover my ears. It was so loud it etched itself in my mind. Don't even get me started on the breathing. The closer the men got to me, the more it felt like they were breathing down my neck. I could hear people talking. I didn't recognize the voices, but people were discussing, trying to find the group and me.

"These stupid kids are messing everything up!" One whisper said.

"We will capture them, Lieutenant," another answered.

"We'll kill them if we need to!" A third added.

I took a moment to catch my breath. I slammed my feet down on the ground and ran once more. No matter the distance between myself and whoever was chasing me, the sounds got louder. My ears and my head hurt so much. I started to feel something trickle down the side of my neck, but I didn't care at this moment in time. I wanted to get as far away as I could. I just want some peace of mind from these loud noises that shouldn't be loud. Why is this happening to me?

While I ran, something caught my ear's attention. It was something new. Behind all the loud noises of the soldiers in the woods, which shouldn't have been this loud, I heard my name.

"Cricket?" A voice spoke.

The voice was a reasonable distance away as it wasn't ear-piercing to me. That thick Russian accent couldn't be anyone other than Rocket. I followed his voice, and the louder it got, the closer I was to finding him.

"Rocket, where are you?" I whisper-yelled.

"Up here!" Rocket replied. I looked up to see Rocket sitting on a high-up tree branch. "Get up here, Crick!"

I climbed the tree, sitting next to him, and realized his wings were gone. How did he figure that out?

"God, you have no idea how happy I am to see you!" I hugged Rocket quickly.

"Are you okay? You are shaking terribly," Rocket commented.

I looked down at my hand, watching it tremble. "I guess I am," I paused, "dude, the weirdest thing is happening to me."

Rocket looked at me, concerned. "What happened?"

All the worried feelings left my body for a quarter of a second. The only thing I could do was look at Rocket. Even with the anxious emotion on his face, I couldn't help but admire him. His face in the moon's light had shaped him so perfectly. His skin looked porcelain, so smooth and beautiful. If I could, I could watch Rocket's radiating allurement forever.

He is so charming, I thought, then quickly shook it out of my mind.

"Everything is so loud. The sounds are hurting my brain," I confided Rocket.

He looked at me with more confusion. "What sounds, Cricket?"

"Everything! Echoes of footsteps, breathing, leaves and twigs crunching, people's whispers. These sounds are on full blast in my head. It's as if my hearing went from zero to a hundred when we entered the forest. Everything hurt so much, Rocket," I explained. I pressed my hands over my ears, hoping something would work. It didn't.

"I'm here. I am right here." He grabbed my head and pulled me to his chest.

Once he did that, my face became warm. I was so close to him that I could hear his heartbeat grow faster. Tears formed in my eyes, and I couldn't stop some of them from running down my cheek. I let go of my ears and hugged Rocket tightly. We sat like that until I started to feel awkward and sat up. When going to wipe my face of tears, I noticed something on my hand. It was cold, wet, and dark in color. I pandered at my palms. Was that *blood*?

My stomach dropped, and my heart raced in my chest. "Rocket, I think there is blood on me..."

"Blood?" Rocket took my hands and moved them into the moon's light. I was right. It was blood. "Jesus, where did it come from?" He looked up at me, grabbed my jaw with one of his hands, and turned my head.

"What is it, Rocket?" I asked him, but he went silent. "Keith, answer me. What is it?" I touched the side of my face with my fingertips and looked down at it. More blood appeared on my hand.

"You're bleeding from your ears." Rocket's eyes showed terror.

"Oh, fuck!" I blurt out.

Rocket covered my mouth with his hand. "Don't get us caught," he then uncovered my mouth. "It will be okay. It's probably from the loud sounds you are hearing now. You probably injured your eardrum," Rocket rummaged through his pockets and took his handkerchief from his jeans pocket. He gently pressed it against my ear and cleaned the blood that ran down my neck on both sides.

"I had to have ruptured my eardrums. How can I still hear after all of this?" I asked.

"I don't know. Maybe it is your power," Rocket replied as he cared for my injuries.

"My power? If this is the power I got, I was cheated out of luck. In any case, you and Moss have at least cooler powers," I crossed my arms.

"Crick, Moss almost strangled herself while she was sleeping. I could tell by the mark on her neck. My wings, though beautiful, are painful when they appear and disappear like my skin is ripping open." Rocket looked at me, "We all got cheated out of luck."

I sat awkwardly, "I didn't mean to make it sound like I have it worse than you guys. I'm sorry, Rocket."

"It's alright. Welcome to our club now!" A snarky smirk appeared on his face.

My heart fluttered as we just sat there, Rocket's hand still holding onto the side of my face with the handkerchief. I quickly realized how close we *really* were to each other. There was barely a foot difference. Looking at him was like looking at the stars. Not just any star, well, not a star at all, but a *nebula*, the *Sharpless-279 Nebula*, to be specific. I learned about it in science class last year. Other than history, I enjoyed Earth Science a lot. My favorite part of that class was learning about the stars and planets. Since I've seen this fantastic cloud of gas and debris, I picture Rocket in my mind for some reason. Maybe it's the colors. My oh my, he is as handsome as the Sharpless Nebula.

I snapped back into focus when I heard another voice from a distance, my cheeks still red and hot from my thoughts.

"Did you hear that?" I asked Rocket.

He looked at me with a funny face. "I don't have cricket-superhero hearing, dude. What do you hear?"

I rolled my eyes at him. "Oh, shut up," I listened intently to make out whose voice it might be. "I think it's Moss. She's probably looking for us."

"Alright, let's get down and find her. But be careful, you are bleeding again," Rocket wiped the side of my face once more. "Here, take it. If it happens again." He gave me the handkerchief while we carefully descended from the tree.

"Thanks," I replied, jumping to the ground. We then started to make our way over to Moss by my hearing alone.

Was this my power? Cricket super hearing? This can't be all of it, right? I didn't even know cricket hearing was like this. Maybe it isn't even like this at all. How should I know? I guess when you're a blind little cricket, you have to find another way to get around, and I guess that means excellent ears. Now thinking of it, Mourn mentioned that when one of your senses can't be used, your other senses heighten. I guess I have to think a lot before coming to any conclusions.

It took us a good while to locate Moss. She was with MariGold, Clover, and Peep.

From what I was told, Clover was looking for the rest of the group from the sky for an easy sight.

"Wasma and Acorn are about a mile away from where we are now, but I can't find Darwin anywhere, so we need to search further for him," Clover said, picking up Peep. She then flew up a couple of feet in the air as we followed her on foot.

Just like she said, we found Wasma and Acorn in no time. Now, the only one left was Darwin. I hope he is doing alright out here by himself. He should be okay, right?

Darwin Pakún

PART ONE

Chapter 8
Fear The Human
Shadow

*P*rophecies are the worst, especially when they concern your future. I wish Mom had never told me mine. I'd probably sleep easier at night if she hadn't.

Growing up in the South Wing wasn't always bad, but it's still hard to think of when everything was normal. Living here is now hell. The Humans started forcing us to use a form of dark magic, which is known to be deadly and even make people go insane. The days always felt so long. I would be with my mom in the early mornings as her caretaker. She had grown very ill at the beginning of my teen years, and with no dad around to help her, I took on this tiring job. Then, when the sun rose, I had to get to work in the potion shops. It was the most dangerous job they gave in the South Wing. Potions would explode sometimes and cause people to get sick, injured, or even die. I've witnessed people dropping dead on many occasions and being dragged away by the Humans. There was only one reason I didn't lose myself there: I knew Wasma would be by my side. Wasma, though I like calling her Waszy, is my best friend. We have known each other for around ten years and are inseparable. She made my life worth living and showed me that there are still people who can make me happy.

I don't want to think about all the horrible things I've been through, but something needs to be said. I never speak of my prophecy, the one I told the group in the tunnels, because I don't like the looks I get when I do. Usually, people reply with pity or fear. It's nothing good to me nor worth the pain it causes me.

While we were running away from the TreeTrunk Motel and being chased by Humans, I collapsed to the forest floor. I don't remember when I hit the dirt. I only remember panicking when darkness swarmed around me, and everything went black. My eyes opened, but I wasn't in the forest anymore. I knew this place way too well. It was my 'mind palace'. Some kids grow out of their imagination, and some are cursed by it forever. I am one of those kids. But this wasn't any type of mind palace where everything is happiness. It was like a waiting room full of my most hated memories. Well, it literally was a waiting room.

"No. Why is this happening again?" I said into the empty room.

The walls were greenish gray with white stripes going vertical. I despised this room for many reasons. One was the striped walls that gave the room a stale smell, and the second reason was that this room was where the residents of the South Wing had to go when Humans took over. I remember that day well. I stood behind Mom and her wheelchair as others filled the seats around us. We were only there for a check-up by some Human doctors to see if we were healthy enough to work in the shops. Mom and I were waiting for hours to see the doctors. When we finally got a room, they clarified that Mom wasn't able to work because of her disabilities, but I was. They made me fill out forms and told us to go home, and I'd be summoned the next day for work. From that day forward, I knew life would be different.

Now I'm back in that same waiting room, not literally but mentally.

I waited, sitting in one of the uncomfortable chairs, knowing what would happen next now that I was here.

A door swings open, and a whisper calls my name, "... Darwin..."

Like always, my body lifted off the chair and I followed the voice. Even if I tried to fight it to sit back down, I couldn't. I walked over to the door and went through it. From that point on, I am no longer in the waiting room. I stand in a void of flashing memories while that same whisper tries to talk to me. My body leads me from memory to memory. They were on display as if my traumas and experiences were art at a museum to look at for *'fun.'* Nothing was all that bad at first. It showed me my mom in the medical center after she had a stroke, the time when Wasma's dad chased me out of their house, and, of course, more. But there was a new one that I was drawn to. It was something from a couple of years ago. Looking at this one made my spine shiver. I remember this one too well.

"Is this necessary?!" I yelled. I knew who I was yelling at. It was always there, lurking in the darkness.

More whispers were spoken, but I couldn't understand them this time.

"You're useless, you know!" I shouted back.

I was forced to look at the memory. Even if I wanted to, I couldn't ignore it. It was about my powers. The first time this all happened. Wasma was the one to find me on the ground unconscious. I hurt her that day. Though it was an accident, I terrified her. She yelled for me to wake up, and every time she touched my skin, she got burned as if I were a powered-on stove. That's when *the shadow* first appeared. It started to swing at Wasma like she was a danger to me. When I eventually woke up, she refused to talk to me for a week. When she was ready, we talked about it, and she forgave me. I couldn't forgive myself, though. I hurt my only friend in that state. Wasma still has burn marks on her hands from that day, and I feel guilty whenever I see them.

Everyone wonders why I always prefer not to use my powers. The reason is that I harm others when it comes out. The prophecy and my powers are all a curse to me that I must live with daily. At some point, I started to refer to my curse as the Human Shadow. This curse has gotten stronger over the years and has become more challenging to control.

When I mentioned to Wasma that I wanted more control over the curse, the shadow, and everything, she agreed to help me.

I'd be locked in a room away from others, forcing the shadow out of my body. Our theory was that the Human Shadow controlled everything, like a parasite. She said that it would be easier to deal with if I could either work with it or control it. So, the experiment began. Those weeks were full of hardships and sleepless nights. The Human Shadow would manipulate me and overpower my body.

But, one day, we had success. I was able to summon and retract the shadow with ease. Since then, the Human Shadow and I worked together instead of dominating each other. But sometimes, it will come out and make me its puppet, as it is now.

"Human Shadow, why are you doing this to me? We made a deal we would work together, not separate, you parasite!" I yelled.

"You need to get used to it, Dar," the Human Shadow appeared.

"What have I said about using the name for me? You are not allowed to call me that," I spoke sternly.

"You called me a parasite! And I don't care what you ask of me. You need to understand I'm doing this to help you," Human Shadow replied.

"Help with what?"

"The war, Darwin. The prophecy. Did you forget? I can remind you."

"No need for that–" I was interrupted by the shadow.

"A war will come to thee, and you will become a beacon for the shadows of the void to use to enter the Mainland. No power, no nothing. You will just be a beacon for them to come and slaughter." The Human Shadow's voice became deeper, more menacing as it quoted the prophecy.

My body felt cold, like all the blood was drained out of me. I knew that prophecy would bite me in the ass, but I didn't think it would come so soon. I was only made to be the beacon for the shadows of the void to enter through, and that's it.

"Thanks," I rolled my eyes.

"Anytime! Seriously, now, I only do this so you can get accustomed to this feeling. I don't need our beacon harmed when we all come out," the Human Shadow explained.

"Well, at least you could have given me a warning!" I yelled at it.

"How the hell would I do such a thing! This was the warning! The 'war' is coming closer than you believe it is," it yelled back at me.

I stood there silent, "I got the message then. Just let me go back."

"Fine. But you must tell the others sooner or later before it's too late, or maybe it is already too late." The Shadow passed me, and my spine straightened from the sense of dread that fumed from it.

Before I could reply, I woke up with a light in my eyes. When the light left my vision, I saw Acorn holding a small, bright bottle in his hands. Wasma probably gave it to him so he could check me out. It took a second for everything to focus when I noticed everyone was there, all circling me. I shot up from the ground.

"What happened? We were looking for you and found you on the floor passed out," Cricket was the first to speak.

"Not to mention that an actual shadow loomed over your body. And when I tried to grab on to you, your skin was burning hot!" Acorn adds.

I looked over to Wasma. She gave me that look. The look of *it happened again, didn't it?* "Guys, get out of his face so he can relax for a second! Lord Elders! He's fine now. We should get going before the Humans try to catch us again," Wasma demanded to the others.

Wasma gave me her hand to help me up fully. Once I was, we began the walk through the dark forest, with Wasma treading next to me.

"We're getting close to it, aren't we? The so-called war?" Wasma's voice was cold like stone.

"Yeah, we are," I replied to my best friend, putting my hands in my jeans pockets as we walked the rest of the way in silence.

War was coming soon, and the Human Shadow was the first warning.

Gregory Mont

Chapter 9
Where Are You?

*F*our thirty a.m., my alarm clock read as I hit the off button. It's always a pain to make that ancient thing stop beeping. I'm surprised I haven't thrown it across the room yet to shut it up. Oh, wait, I have done that many times, and it still works.

Every morning is like the other. I make my lonely queen-sized bed, take a quick shower to wake myself up, brush my teeth, and get dressed into my work uniform. My clothes are always laid out on my desk from the night before. I slip on my gray button-up collared shirt, navy blue tie, black dress pants, and black leather Oxford shoes.

Besides the small light in the kitchen by the coffee maker, the house is dark. I pour myself a mug of hot black coffee and stand by the counter, just thinking. Last night was a wreck. First, I had to deal with my ex-wife, Catherine, over the phone because she now wants to see Cricket. I wouldn't have a problem with her seeing him, but there is, and it's a lot. She was (still is) an alcoholic, and in the earlier days of Cricket's childhood, she was also a heroin user. When Cricket was born, he was addicted to opioids. So, I can say in my own words that she was very neglectful of our son. We always got into more verbal than physical fights, but there were still times when she did hit. She's the type of woman who doesn't care if she hurts people, even if it's her own flesh and blood. A memory traces my mind: Valentine's Day of 1977, five months before Cricket turned nine. He had just come home with Catherine from the subway after school. I remember his face lit up when he saw me home early from work.

*****

"Dad! What are you doing at home?" He ran up to hug me.

"I wanted to surprise my family for a fun Valentine's Day dinner," I told my son. The smile on his face was so innocent then. "So how was school, Sport? Did you get any Valentine's?"

Cricket nodded quickly, pulling my hand to the coffee table. Catherine was now on the couch, holding her third glass of red wine of the day, and just lit a cigarette.

"Honey, Cricket's home. Put out the cigarette," I told her, opening the windows. She rolled her eyes and put the cigarette out on the ashtray.

Cricket grabbed a big brown bag from his backpack and spilled it on the coffee table. "Mrs. K said we couldn't open them in class because the candy would 'bring more bugs in this God-forsaken classroom,'" Cricket mocked his teacher's voice with his lisp.

I sat on the rugged floor to help him open his Valentine's. "Cricket, I didn't know the whole school was your friend," I joked as I separated the candy from the cards.

We spent a good fifteen minutes going through everything. My eyes wandered to Cricket, and I noticed a pink sheet of paper on his lap. "What's that, Sport? Is it from a secret admirer?" I whispered, smiling at my son.

He smiled sweetly, "Yeah, but it's not very secret because it has a name on it. I opened this one in the bathroom at school when I saw it in my mailbox."

"Can I see it?" I always gave him space to let him start making boundaries for himself.

"Hm, okay," Cricket gave me the folded paper. I opened it and started reading;

'Hi, Cricket! happy ~~valintynes~~ *valentine's day! you're my best friend and i really like you! i hope we can hang out again soon! my Mom said i can ask you to be my* ~~valintynes~~ *valentine, please?*

–Luke'

My eyes widened, and I looked over at my son and then back at the letter. There isn't anything wrong with the letter or the sender. I was just a bit shocked when I first read it. "Cricket, can we talk in your room for a second?" I asked him. He looked up at me with a bit of worry in his eyes. He probably thinks he is in trouble, which he isn't.

I made sure the door was closed behind us before I started to speak, "Okay, so you aren't in any trouble. I'm not mad with the letter or that it comes from a boy, either. But I need to tell you something. This world isn't very kind to some people, and sadly, this is one of those things. If you like this boy, which I am perfectly fine with, you need to know something. For future reference, telling people you do isn't always the safest. For example, with Mama, she—she doesn't understand it. Sometimes, when people don't understand, they can say mean stuff. Okay? I love you and always will. No matter what." I try not to cry in front of my son, but it's hard to look at his face like this. He looked paler, and his eyes were misty. I hugged Cricket tight. I had known this situation very well from my own years, and I wanted to make sure he knew I loved him.

As we left his room, we were greeted by a very tipsy Catherine. She held an empty bottle of wine in one hand and a pink piece of paper in the other. That should have been my cue to grab my son and run, but I didn't know what would happen then. Catherine turned to Cricket and me and started to yell. Most of it was about 'God's plan' and that our son would burn in the fires of Hell if he continued this path of life. She spoke about him as if he wasn't eight years old but was a fully grown man. It's so ironic that all of this happened moments after each other. It's as if she just wanted to prove what I was saying to Cricket was right.

"Catherine, calm down. Can we talk about this? You're scaring our son," I pleaded.

By her face, I could tell she was pissed. "My son, taken advantage of by the Devil's work! How do you wish to explain that, Greg? The Devil has cursed our home and made my son a queer. A fag!" She yelled.

I tried my best to cover Cricket's ears from these harmful words, but she said it loud enough for our neighbors to hear.

*****

I can't even remember or want to remember what was said during the fight. All I tried to do was keep her away from *my* son. I can still hear his sobs from when he was hiding behind me.

Somehow, she got her hands on Cricket, and that's when the first hits were shot. She slapped him across the face. I was full of rage, and all I could see was red. My hand grabbed my wife's arm, and that's when I hit her. She let go of Cricket, and once he was out of her grasp, he ran to his room, bawling his eyes out.

Everything after that was a blur. The only thing I remember saying was, *"Don't you dare put your hands on my son ever again, you drunken bitch!"* A neighbor heard the yelling and called the cops. We were both arrested that night, but my charges were dropped as they were in self-defense for my minor son. Catherine got a year in jail and no visitation till she got herself together and stopped using drugs and excessive drinking. I fought tooth and nail with the courts to get full custody of Cricket. Once I won, we moved to LongEdge, Ohio.

Even though it was years ago, it still fills my body with anger to this day. I can even remember the bruise on his cheek she'd given him. Now, he has to go back to a person who hates him for the rest of the summer. She even has him for his 17th birthday—the day I helped plan for Cricket, his friends, and me.

I continue to think as I finally move over to Cricket's door, as I do every morning. Every morning, I go to Cricket's room, kiss his forehead, and make my way to work quietly, as he usually is still sleeping. I look at his bedroom door, now thinking about the argument from the night before.

"Today's a new day, Greg. He is your son, after all. He can't be mad at you forever," I open the door quietly, peeking my head in. As I did, I saw that his bed was empty. "Cricket? Cricket!" I raised my voice, putting my mug down on his dresser. The room was empty. His backpack, Walkman, Walkie-Talkie, and wool jacket were gone. Everything important to my son was gone. Panic ran through my body. What happened to my son? I looked over at Cricket's desk. A piece of paper was neatly folded under a rock. I opened it, and it was a letter from Cricket. My eyes frantically traced through the paper. It said he would be at Rocket's house. I let out a loud sigh as I exited his room with relief. This hadn't been the first time he'd snuck out and gone to his friend's house for the night.

I went to the kitchen to call the Chili residence. Yes, I knew he would be safe if he were at Rocket's house, but I just wanted to put my mind at ease.

"Hello? Who dis'?" A sleepy-sounding woman with a thick Russian accent answered the phone.

"Hello Margaret, it's Gregory Mont, Cricket's father. I'm sorry for waking you at this hour, but is Cricket over at your place? I went to check on him, but he wasn't there. He made a letter for me that said he was going to *Roc*-Keith's house for the rest of the night. Is he there by any chance?" I quickly rant. I only wanted to know that he made it there fine and that he had just crashed on their couch for the night or that he was passed out in Rocket's bed next to him. At least let them tell me he is safe.

"Wait, I thought Keith was with Cricket at your home?—Ivan!" Margaret started speaking in her native language to her husband. For how long I've known the Chili family, I wish I had started to pick up the language. She came back to the phone. "You ask Moss's parents, Greg?" Margaret asked me.

My mouth felt dry, and my heart fell out of my body. *Wasn't he there? He has to be, right?* I choked out my words. "No, I haven't. Let me call them real quick."

"Alright. When you get an answer, call us," the Russian woman told me.

I hung up, and my fingers rapidly dialed the number of the Brine family. Waiting for them to pick up felt like it took twenty years. But when they did, I asked the same question.

131

"No, Cricket isn't here, and neither is Rocket," Mitchel Brine, Moss's dad, said.

I swallowed hard, "Can you please ask Moss if she knows anything?"

"Yeah, I totally can." I heard Mitchel getting out of bed and walking to Moss's room. He knocked on the door. "Moss, can I come in?" He paused. "Moss?" A door creaked, and I heard the sound of a father's life shatter. "Moss!"

"Mitchel, what's going on?"

"She's not here. Where the *fuck* is my daughter?! Nadia! Moss is missing!"

Rocket, Moss, and Cricket were gone. I didn't know what to tell the other worried parents.

"Mitchel, listen to me. We will all figure this out, but we must work together here, okay? Get to my house now, and we will get this all straightened out," I told him.

"Okay, we will be there right away," Mitchel spoke out of breath.

I called Margaret back and told her the same thing, and within ten minutes, two cars pulled up in my driveway. I ran over to the front door to let them in.

"Where the hell are our kids, Greg? I know they can sneak out sometimes, but they always end up at one of our houses," Nadia, Moss's mom, said. She was holding her eight-month-old baby, Judy, as she paced my living room.

"I have no clue, Nadia. This isn't like them," I replied.

"We should call the cops. Don't you have friends on the inside that could help us, Greg?" Mitchel asked.

"I do. I'll go make the call," I rushed back to the kitchen, grabbed the telephone, and dialed our town's police.

"Hello, this is the LongEdge Police Department. What is your emergency?" A woman answered the phone.

"Hello, my name is Gregory Mont. I live at 1167 Birdcage Road in LongEdge. I need to speak to Sergeant Jones now. My son and his two friends have gone missing. Please, this is urgent."

Three cop cars took an hour and a half to drive to my home. Three of the six men were inside looking around, two were outside, and one—Mr. Sergeant Jason Jones himself— sat at my dinner table asking us questions.

I paced my kitchen as he interviewed me.

"Greg, please calm down. They're teens! They probably snuck out for a party or to drink and smoke weed in a park somewhere," Sergeant Jones said.

"Don't tell me to be calm when my kid is missing! And to be clear, you don't know my son, Jason! He isn't like other teens, and neither are his friends. Cricket's only friends are Roc- Keith, and Moss. He doesn't talk to many other kids. He doesn't even like big parties. So don't you dare say my son is doing anything like drugs or drinking," I pointed my finger at him, slamming my other hand down on the table. My nerves were all over the place. How dare he say something like that. Jason knew about my ex-wife from all the times we would hang out at the bar after work. Ivan puts a hand on my shoulder. I took a step back, "He always despised all that stuff. And you, of all people, should know why."

I sat down in front of Jason, "Cricket was supposed to get on a plane today and go with Catherine for the summer if that's anything important. He wasn't happy to hear that he was forced to be with her," I rub my hands over my face.

"That definitely helps. Does she have a number we can use to contact her?" Sergeant Jones asked. I nod. He gave me a piece of paper to write the number down on. After I did, another officer took the paper and went to my phone to call her.

"You mentioned your son, Cricket, and his friends, Keith and Moss aren't like other teens. What do you mean about that?" The Sergeant asked.

I looked at Nadia with desperate eyes, and then I looked over at Margaret and Ivan.

I think Nadia sees the worry on my face as she looks over at Rocket's parents, too. "Hey, let's go into the living room and give Greg room to breathe." Nadia had put her arm around Margaret's shoulders, and they slowly walked out of the kitchen. I turned back to the Sergeant.

From what Cricket told me, Ivan and Margaret are strict at home. It's shocking, as Rocket is a huge metalhead, and his dad takes him to every metal and punk concert ever. They aren't the most accepting people in the world, though. Everyone was surprised when they didn't overreact when Moss came out as a transsexual. I believe it's referred to as being transgender now, but that's just the phrase I grew up hearing. Anyway, all I know is Rocket's parents have mentioned a lot about his future. As if it's a story they wrote instead of him living it. Cricket said they want Rocket to marry a beautiful Russian woman and have many kids. From what my son has told me and what I've seen, Rocket should be the last person on Earth to have kids. He hates them with a burning passion. Even if he was good with kids, Cricket has mentioned the face he makes when kids get brought into the conversation about the future.

"I don't tell many people this for safety reasons, but my son, well," I sighed, "he swings the same way if that makes sense. And so do his friends, from what I've noticed and know. They never had a lot of friends. It's been the three of them since we moved here. Our world is so corrupted that my son, Cricket, and his friends can't be themselves. And when they are themselves, they get ridiculed for it," I whispered to the man. He was writing a lot in his notes. I wonder how many slurs he threw in there after I said that. Jason was known for using derogatory words towards people, at least when we were closer.

The other officer returned from the phone, "Your ex-wife wants to speak with you, Lieutenant."

"No need to call me that," I said as I excused myself and walked over to the phone. I dread every time I have to speak with this woman.

I grabbed the phone and answered it, "Hello Catherine."

"Gregory! Our son, where is our son!" Her voice was panicked.

"You mean *my* son, Catherine. You never gave two shits about him till yesterday."

"Greg, what are you talking about–" I interrupted Catherine.

"I have done everything for him for the past eight years. So, don't you say he is *our* son? He is *my* son." I spoke sternly towards my ex-wife. She tried to argue back, but I wasn't done, "I wouldn't need to call you about this if you were here in his life. He is missing, for God's sake! Now get your head out of your ass, Catherine, and be a mother for once in your life. Like Cricket said last night, you can't do anything when you're five hundred miles away."

The line went quiet. "I'm packing something quickly right now, Greg. Our son could be in danger. Who knows what kind of people might take a child, God forbid, if that is the case. I will get the next flight to Ohio, I promise," her voice was flat.

"Good. Good to know you finally have your head screwed on somewhat the right way. Maybe that new marriage of yours is helping," I commented bitterly, hanging up the phone.

When I returned to the dining room, I saw Nadia and Mitchel talking to Sergeant Jones at the table. From the front of the house, I heard the door open. Doug, Rocket's older brother, had arrived.

"I came as soon as I could when I heard what happened. How are you holding up mom, dad?" I overheard Doug say as he ran to his parents. I've met Doug on many occasions; he is a great person. He would always offer to take the three kids to the mall and drive-ins all the time. Cricket has even mentioned that Doug was like an older brother to him.

When Nadia and Mitchel finished talking to Jason, the Chili's went into the kitchen to speak next.

"Yeah, Keith. Well, we call him Rocket. He can be a huge doofus sometimes, but he is never this stupid not to come home," Doug told the Sergeant.

"Is there anywhere he would be, like a shop or hangout place?" Jason asked.

"No, I don't think so. Margaret?" Ivan asked his wife.

"That I know of? No, I don't," Mrs. Chili said.

"Yes, there is, actually," Doug looked at his parents. "Rocket and his friends always hang out in the woods behind this house. I believe in this run-down car. I only know about it because I had to get Rocket from there once. But him getting lost there, there's no chance he would. The same goes for Cricket and Moss," Doug said.

"Can you elaborate on that?" Sergeant Jones asked as he intensively wrote.

"Well, they know the woods as if it were like remembering that one line from a movie. They have been there probably millions of times in the past five years or so," Doug explained.

"Gregory, do you know of this run-down car?" Asked the Sergeant.

"No, I never really go into the woods other than for firewood," I told honestly.

"It makes sense, as it's not really on your property. The woods, your property ends in the middle or so of it. The car is over the property line, which I believe is state-owned. It's pretty safe there, honestly. A fence surrounds the government property, but one part isn't fenced off. That's where your property and the state's property connect. At least that's what Rocket told me." Doug looked at his hands, picking at them.

"This is vital information, Doug. Thank you." The Sergeant said, getting up, "We will start a community search for your children in the woods. Officer Hills, get a group of people together to start a search. Stat. Do any of you have any recent photos of the children?"

"Yes, I do. I have one from the 4th of July on my fridge," I rushed to get the Polaroid. I looked at the photo momentarily, then gave it to the cops. Oh, Cricket, where could you be?

Chapter 10
Mama's Home

*I*t had been five hours since I realized Cricket was gone. More police cars came to my house, and some went to the Chili and Brine residences to look for evidence of their disappearance. I sat on my couch with my hands on the back of my head and my head on my knees. My back straightened when I heard loud knocks on my front door. I got up to open it, thinking it was more officers. That's when I came face to face with Catherine. She was standing next to a tall man who looked at least seven years older than she was.

"I promised to get the first flight here, and I did. The airport was a mess of its own, though. Not to mention having to get a rental car. People don't give a shit here, do they?" Catherine looked up at me.

She looked the same since the last time I saw her in person. Her long brown hair was a mess, and so was her makeup. I'd be surprised if it were from her crying. She wasn't the type to cry. Even when Cricket was born and brought to her, not even tears of joy left her eyes. I always had the feeling she was heartless. But it's been almost eight years. Maybe she grew one? I'm not getting my hopes up, though.

"Well, the people here aren't the best with others passing through. At least you got here in time. The search will be starting around eleven, starting here. I hope you packed sneakers in your bag," I looked down at her feet as she wore heels. How like her.

"Yes, I did," she snipped, "it's not like I am Speedy Gonzales. I can't click my heels together and arrive at your house in five seconds like you wished I could." I could sense the sarcasm in her voice. The man behind her grabbed Catherine's shoulder to pull her away from my face.

"Maybe this wouldn't have happened if you were in his life. If you had called once in a while when you weren't drunk, that would have helped a lot. But that's not even why he doesn't like you. You know that, and you know why." I moved my face closer to hers, lowering my voice but trying to stay calm. "As for what all of us know, he's missing because he didn't want to go with you, Catherine."

The man behind Cathrine looked at me. I knew what he was trying to say: *'Let's not do this right now.'* Stepping back from Catherine, I faced the man.

"You must be the new husband. I'm Gregory, Catherine's ex-husband and father of Cricket. It's a pleasure to meet you," I said, reaching out to shake his hand.

"Yes, I'm James McLee. It's a pleasure to meet you too, but a horrible way to first meet." James shakes my hand with a sympathetic smile. He doesn't seem like a guy Catherine would like, but I guess he helps balance her personality by being nice.

I let them inside. My ex-wife and her new husband went to the couch to sit with Nadia while I entered the kitchen.

"I either need a shot of vodka or a shotgun to take me out of this misery," I say through my teeth.

Mitchel was standing by the counter with baby Judy in his arms, "And if you choose the shotgun, I'll be there to take in Cricket if needed. He is already like a son to me and a brother to Moss." He joked, pulling a warm bottle of milk out of the microwave for the baby.

I chuckle at his joke, "Who says it was for myself?"

"I see you hate her. Understandably, at least to a point," Mitchel replies.

"You have no idea," I answered, looking at him. I grabbed the coffee pot and filled some cups for everyone. "Ivan, Margaret, coffee?" I gestured to them. They said yes as they came over to get their mugs. Then, I gave Mitchel and his wife a refill of tea.

I went over to Catherine with the last two mugs. "I believe you still take your coffee black, and I didn't know how you take yours, James," I mentioned.

"This is fine, thank you," James smiled, grabbing it. Catherine then thanked me as well. I went back to the kitchen to stand next to Mitchel again. He was the only person I wanted to be near at this moment.

It felt like we were just waiting for our kids to open the front door and say they got lost in the woods and were safe and not hurt. What if they did get hurt? I'd look like a terrible father to the police and the courts. It's not like they don't already think that. I try my best as a single father. I don't know what to do without my son. He is my only hope for this world. I just want him home... *Why can't I wake up from this nightmare?*

My ears perked up when Catherine started to speak to Nadia.

"Your daughter Moss, well, she sounds like a great kid. I hope we find them so I can finally have the chance to meet her," Catherine said in a flat voice.

A chuckle leaves my mouth. Everyone turns to me, "Catherine, when the hell did you start caring about Cricket's friends?"

Her eyes widened, "Excuse me, I have no idea what you're talking about."

"Greg, what do you mean?" Nadia's face shot over to mine.

"Well, if I remember correctly, Cricket told me you never cared for his friends. You said you didn't think they were good influences on him," my words made everything quiet. I took a sip of my coffee.

Nadia looked at my ex-wife, stunned. "Did you seriously say that?"

"Oh, Mrs. Brine, I'd never say anything like that!" Catherine tries to defend herself.

"I wasn't born yesterday," Nadia smacked her lips together, "And the slip-ups. I thought when you called Moss *'he'* it was an accident, but I'm guessing it wasn't, was it?" Nadia tried to get up from the couch when Catherine grabbed her arm.

"Nadia, wait one second. Please, I promise I wasn't doing it on purpose. You know how hard these things can be. Switching from he to she? It's confusing,"

"Don't touch me," she turned to Catherine, "And no, it isn't at all. When I look at my *daughter*, I see my little girl. When I look at my adult son, I see my little boy. My *daughters* and my son are my world, and I love them equally. I should have known from Greg's words alone and all the times he had to apologize for you when you would call when Moss was over. She'd hear you say such cruel things. Doesn't she have to deal with enough in life already?... I need a smoke." She snatched her arm back and walked out the front door.

I don't blame her for her anger. Even if I didn't know Catherine was calling Moss *'he'* by *'accident'*, I knew about the other stuff. I'm always apologizing for her rudeness. Mitchel followed his wife outside, with Judy sleeping in his arms. Then, Catherine stormed out the back door, with James following her like a puppy.

"My Lord," I sat on the couch, resting my face in my hands.

Minutes later, I heard a baby crying. Mitchel walked in from outside, "Do you have a place I could change her?"

"Of course," I showed him to my room, "You can change her on my bed."

I was about to leave before Mitchel said something. "Your ex-wife. How did you meet?" He was generally asking.

I stepped back inside, closing the door, my back against it. "We met in high school after I moved from Georgia to New York with my parents. I was 17, she was 18, and it was the '50s. We were the typical high school sweethearts. I should have listened to my mom when she said high school relationships were just puppy love. That should have been my warning, but we loved each other too much. Well, it was more like *I* loved her too much. We got married at 22, and she then got pregnant with Cricket. By that time, she was sneaking heroin and all other types of opioids that I didn't fully know about at the time. Then everything got worse. She started to drink and didn't even try to hide her heroin use anymore. She would chain smoke cigarettes or marijuana a lot in the house. Catherine would have outbursts of rage and would break things. Thankfully, she didn't touch Cricket until," I paused. "Well, I've told you..." I took a second, looking at the floor, "Long story short, she went to jail, and she had no custody or visitation until she got herself clean... I'm sorry for starting shit out there. I'm all over the place right now, so please forgive me."

Mitchel nodded in response. "I get it. Our kids are missing, and Catherine being here doesn't help the stress on you or anyone else. You blame her. We both know that you married a narcissist." He picked up Judy, laying her against his shoulder. "I used to think like Catherine when coming to Moss. I didn't take Moss's coming out the best, and I was a horrible father back then. We got into arguments upon arguments because I wanted my son and thought that a right of mine was being taken from me. I wasn't thinking clearly until Nadia talked to me, and she was right, of course. That woman is an absolute treasure, I'll tell you that. So, after a bit of thinking and time, I decided to be in my daughter's life to help her, not hurt her. Though she isn't my little boy anymore, I can still teach my daughter to grill, build, and do anything I want my child to learn. And even though she doesn't like football or any 'boy' things, we can still connect. She is my little princess now, and I love her."

I smiled at Mitchel, "At least she has two loving parents."

"Yeah, she does. But so can Cricket. I can't tell you to stop hating Catherine. Believe me, I don't like her either, but she came here for Cricket. You have to work together and not against each other, at least for right now," he explained.

"You're right, Mitchel. She came here for our son. I was being immature out there," I replied. We just smiled at each other briefly until Ivan opened the door.

"Search party is here. Let's get our kids," Ivan said. We left the room and rushed outside.

Everyone met in the backyard. There were around thirty people and eleven cops or so on my lawn. "Everyone! You all were given a picture of the kids. The one with red and black hair, that's Keith or Rocket, as people call him. The one with blond braids is Moss. And the boy with brown hair and white patches in it is Cricket. The last place they were estimated to be was by a run-down, abandoned car in the forest. We won't stop searching till we find these kids!" Sergeant Jones shouted through a megaphone. That's when everyone started to move into the forest.

I walked next to Catherine with Milo on his leash. "You think he will help, Greg?" Catherine looked down at the dog.

"He used to be an old hunting dog. Maybe he can sniff Cricket out," I replied. She looked worried, with her hand locked with James'.

She took a deep breath, "Greg?"

"What?"

"Can we talk about last night at some point? You're acting-"

"Catherine, we will talk later. Let's just get our son home safely first," I told her.

She smiled uncertainly. "Yeah, you're right. Let's bring our son home."

Cricket Mont

PART TWO

Chapter 11
Fawn's Floraloxies

*O*range light rose from beyond the trees. The sunrises in Union Beria hit in a different way than the ones back home do. At this very moment, every hue of orange could be in the sky, and every star was still visible.

Immediately, when the morning sky started to glow down at us, my mind began to feel clear. The noises that were once dialed up to a million lowered back to normal, and the bleeding stopped.

While we walked, Moss noticed the dried blood on my shirt. "Jesus, Cricket! Did you get hurt?" Moss words her concern.

"Oh, no? Well, technically, yes. I got my powers when we were in the woods. I'll be alright, though. It was just a bit of blood, and my hearing is normal," I replied.

"Wait, you got your powers? What are they?" She pressed.

"Supersonic cricket hearing," Rocket jokes, strolling behind me with his hands in his jacket pockets.

"Ha-ha, says the one with bird wings," I rolled my eyes, now walking backward to look at both Moss and Rocket. "Where are they anyway?"

"I detract them, and it hurt a *lot*," he answered.

"My gods, Rocket. Anyway, so you can hear things normally now?" Moss turned back to me.

"I guess, but it's bizarre. Everything was fine until we got into the forest, and even before that, I felt something was off. Remember when Mourn told us that because she was blind, her other senses were heightened?"

"Yeah, I remember."

"Well, I assume that because I couldn't see anything in the dark; it was like I didn't have my sight. I'm theorizing that's why everything got so loud. It got to the point where I couldn't take it, and my ear drums were injured. The only thing that doesn't make sense is that I can still hear."

Moss nodded as she walked swiftly beside me, "That's pretty cool. Not the bleeding part, but the hearing thing. Is that all you can do, though?"

"I have no clue. I do hope there is more than just this. It's not the coolest thing ever. It just means I can hear when someone's talking about me behind my back," I snicker.

"I guess we have to wait and see," Moss nudged my shoulder, beaming with assurance.

Union Beria's sunrise passed, returning the sky to its blue colors. We were in the heart of the Bewitched Forest, and everything was so peaceful now that we weren't running away from soldiers. I've always loved nature, but this place made it feel so different from home. Besides this being a different realm, the forest felt alive, as if we were surrounded by people—a crowd, even. I watched the trees move back and forth as if the trees were talking to each other, *dancing.* Tree branches waved to us as we passed by. It was indeed a beautiful sight.

The trees distracted me so much that I almost bumped Acorn over. I asked him if he was alright, but he shushed me instead of giving a typical reply. He just stood there, listening for something, looking for something.

"Acorn, what's the meaning of our stop?" MariGold asked him.

"I think I see it," Acorn said.

"See what?" Rocket questioned, and then Acorn shushed him, too.

He waited for a moment, waiting for who knows what. That's when I noticed what he was watching out for. A creature was running by fast, but if you look closely enough, you can see the majority of what it looks like. It was green, or maybe it had some blue in it? Vines and flowers flowed behind it as if it got tangled. The being had long, slim brown legs as well. I think it was a form of bird, but I'm not sure. It had a yellow beak and feathers, but it just felt out of the ordinary. However, now, considering this place isn't normal in any way, I think it fits in pretty well.

After standing there for a bit, a loud, painful shriek was heard. Acorn's body straightened, and he started to run to where the sound was. We all looked at each other. That's when Wasma sighed, "Let's go follow our gnome."

We followed in the direction Acorn ran in, spotting the ginger-haired boy kneeling next to the creature.

"Acorn, what has gotten into—is that a Floraloxy?" MariGold's voice went from stern to bewilderment.

"Yes, it is! This is my first time seeing a real one in person," Acorn replied, taking his bag off his shoulder and some items out of it.

"What's a Floraloxy?" I asked.

"Floraloxies are Union Beria's most special creatures, almost as special as the Tree Guardians and Goddesses. They are extremely protected animals here and are secluded in the forest so that they can thrive. It's against all laws in Union Beria to hunt in the Bewitched Forest, *Article 13 'Protection Act', line 71*. It's illegal to kill anything here, especially Floraloxies. You can be fined hundreds to thousands of Quins and or even be sent to live in confinement for it," Acorn explained.

"Oh, it's like an eagle in the United States then," Rocket mentioned.

"What's an eagle?" Clover's face turned to confusion.

"It doesn't matter right now. Anyway, why did you run to the Floraloxy?" I asked Acorn.

"The poor thing got caught in a thorn bush," Acorn told me, then started talking to the bird. "Hey, it's okay, little guy. I'm just going to cut you out and bandage your leg up." He grabbed a pair of small scissors and cut it free. Then he took surgical bandages and wrapped them around the Floraloxies' injuries.

The Floraloxy started to get up slowly, falling over a bit, and looked up at the Gnomian. Acorn lowered his head to the colorful bird, and the bird returned the head nod.

"Please be careful out here; it's too dangerous," Acorn told the Floraloxy as he got up.

It took a bit for Acorn to process what happened, "Wait. I just met a real Floraloxy!" His body shined with happiness.

"I know, and it acknowledged you! That's like a huge deal, Acorn!" MariGold put her leaf hands on Acorn's shoulder.

A whistle from the east of the forest broke off the conversation. It caught everyone's attention, even the Floraloxies. We all turned our heads in the direction of the noise. From there, I saw someone standing in the middle of the path.

"Hello?" Darwin uttered.

"Sorry if I'm interrupting something. I mean no harm, I promise. I'm just here for the Floraloxy, that's it!" The person moved closer with her hands slightly up. "I am Ruby Bashwin, one of many caretakers of these creatures. This morning, one of our Floraloxies we care for went missing, and it looks like she found you guys. Hello Lilith, you are looking better already, but you must stop running away." The Floraloxy, Lilith, strutted over to Ruby. She then picked her up and smiled at us.

Ruby Bashwin, as she called herself, was a pretty being. She had strawberry-colored hair with brown roots and small antlers growing from her head downwards. Ruby wore a long magenta dress that came off her shoulders, a rope belt, and a satchel across her chest. I assume she must be a fawn of some sort, as her feet were deer hooves, and she had patches of fur on her shoulders. Her complexion was tan but with spots, similar to how a fawn looked in our realm.

"Oh my, I forgot the deer folk cared for these birds. Our apologies for overstepping our line. Lilith was hurt, and Acorn was trying to help her," MariGold told the fawn girl.

"No need to apologize! Thank you for caring for her. She's been very adventurous for some time now, always finding a way to get in trouble. How could I repay you all?" Ruby's voice was sweet and soft.

"Nothing is needed. I'm just happy Lilith is safe and okay," Acorn replied.

"Please let me. I'd like to invite you to our sanctuary, my home, only if you want to.

At least let me get you some tea. All of you look like you have been traveling for a while," Ruby insisted.

"I guess we do deserve a break. All we have been doing is running," Wasma mentioned.

"Great! You can follow me. My home isn't very far away from here," Ruby said, turning to skip the way.

I tread next to Moss as we followed the others. She wasn't talking like she typically was, which meant something was on her mind.

"Is everything okay, Mossie?" I asked her.

"Oh, me? I–I'm doing great, I mean fine!" Moss replied with some stutters. She kept her eyes on Ruby's back.

I started to put some pieces together. "Oh~ I see what your mind is on. She is charming," I smirked.

Moss hit my arm. "Shut up, Crick." She paused, "Can I ask you something?"

"Of course,"

"Do you believe people can fall in love with someone by first looks alone?" Moss's face became flush.

"Don't tell me you're already falling for the fawn. It's only been like ten minutes," I joked.

"No- I just- My heart feels like it's swelling inside from the moment she looked at me. I haven't even said a word to her, but my heart feels like I've spoken to her millions of times. Is that normal?" She spoke low.

My eyes wandered to Ruby and then to Rocket. "I think it's normal. You can't stop your heart from feeling a certain way, even if you haven't fully met," I smiled at her.

"You think so?"

"I know so. Trust me, I know exactly how you feel. Some people are destined to be connected," I looked back at Rocket.

I fell head over heels when we first met, even though I didn't know what that meant at the time. My heart called out to me back then, and now I get it. I just can't dare to act on it.

"You should go and talk to her," I told her.

"I don't know if I have the guts to do so," Moss commented.

"We aren't home. You could have a chance here," I looked into Moss's eyes.

"You're right," Moss smiled back, "You should talk to him as well. Maybe you can have a chance here, too?"

"Thanks, but I think my chances would be too slim, and I don't want to do anything I'll regret," I replied.

"Have you ever thought not telling Rocket would be something you could regret?" She left me with that question as she slid over to Ruby and started to conversate.

Chapter 12
Head Over Heels

*U*pon arriving at Ruby Bashwin's home, we followed a man-made path to the front doors of a cabin. On the outside, it looked like any other cabin you would see in the countryside of Ohio, but instead of a chicken coop, they had a Floraloxy coop flush against the house.

Ruby motioned for us to follow her inside her home. "Mama, Papa, I have some guests!" Ruby called, her voice echoing through the house.

"Oh dear! What have I told you about bringing people over when the house isn't clean!" A woman's voice called back, entering the part of the home the group and I were standing in. The woman was slender, and her cream-colored dress brushed the wooden floor. Over her dress, she was wearing an olive-green apron that looked as if flour was spilled on it from baking. Her hair was tied up in a messy bun on the top of her head, with pieces framing her face.

"Sorry, Mama. I know you're very busy today with the boys and baking," Ruby replied, taking her satchel off.

The woman sighed. "It's alright. I finally got Neo to bed. The twins are out with your father, gathering for dinner. Hudson and Robin are feeding the birds in the pen, and your sister—oh, I'm going to kill her," Ruby's mother said, cleaning her hands with a rag.

"What did Moxie do?" Ruby asked.

"She's been in her room all day and- excuse my language- is being a huge bitch to your father and me," her mother made clear.

Ruby's mom faced us. "Truly sorry about that. I am a very busy woman with a huge family and no time to waste. I was so busy that I forgot to introduce myself. My apologies! I'm Iris, and it is very nice to meet all of you. Ruby dear, may you take them out in the back while I make some tea for our guests and try to clean up this place?" Iris introduced herself, dusting her apron and moving her hands to and fro.

"Of course, Mama. This way, travelers!" Ruby motioned us to a back door, following her onto the back deck.

"You have a beautiful home, Ruby," Clover said, holding Peep in her arms so it didn't track dirt in the house.

"Thank you! It might be small, but it fits all nine of us," Ruby replied.

"Nine?!" Rocket was shocked.

"Yep, I have a lot of siblings. There is Hudson and Robin; they are the oldest," Ruby pointed to the boys feeding the Floraloxies. "Here comes my father and my two other older brothers, Pascal and Reed. They are twins, if you can't tell. My older sister, Moxie, is inside. She might come out later, but I'm not sure. I also have a baby brother named Neo. He's taking his nap at this moment but will be up soon. Then there is me! If you can't tell, I have a lot of brothers. The boys can get very annoying and overprotective, especially over Moxie and I."

"I get it. I have a lot of siblings, too," Acorn mentioned.

"You understand that a house like this can get pretty cramped most times," Ruby chuckled, "Sorry, I'm babbling. Please make ourselves at home." She pulled some chairs out for some of us to sit down. I sat down next to the very smiley Moss as she kept looking at the fawn girl. I wish I could read her mind sometimes, but I don't think I need to to understand her feelings.

Because Moss and I are best friends, she knows almost everything about me, as I do for her. Moss was the first person other than my dad to whom I said that I was gay. It took many years to accept that part of me. I didn't want to prove my mom's thoughts about me being right. The day I told Moss that I was gay, she started to cry. She told me after sobbing for a minute or two that she understood how I felt because she was queer too. We cried to each other for almost an hour that day. From that day forward, we would have sleepovers and hangouts, with only the two of us talking freely. Though I love Rocket, we needed that time to ourselves. It would be awkward to tell the person you like that you have a crush on them face to face. It's just different when you like your best friend in that way.

The idea that I might have a *'thing'* for Rocket was brought up during one of those hangouts. I remember every word she said that night as if it were yesterday.

*****

"You have a crush on Rocket Man?! This is the same Rocket we are both thinking about, right? The boy who got hit in the head by a soccer ball in gym class the other day. Keith

Mason freakin' Chili?!" Moss ate her popcorn while I put the VHS tape in the player.

"Shut up! You know that I'm talking about Rocket. And what's so bad about it if I do, huh?" I snickered back, sitting next to her with the remote.

"It isn't bad, but dude, WHY?!" Moss was being dramatic again.

I rolled my eyes, stealing some of her popcorn.

"Hey, that's mine!" Moss groaned.

"I made it! Also, you were told not to eat popcorn because you now have braces," I stuck my tongue out at her.

"Not my fault that I was screwed over with bad teeth and had to get them. The dentist can't tell me what to do."

"They literally can. As well as your mom and dad."

Moss pushed my arm, "Anyway, seriously now. If you like him, I'll allow it. I can already picture the wedding."

"Why, thank you for the permission, 'Mom,' for the wedding that will never happen," I joked.

"Anything for my child. But I hope you know that if you become an item, I will pre-threaten the bastard if he ever hurts you."

"I know you will, Moss and the same goes for you when you get a girlfriend. If that ever happens."

"I'm dying single. What are you talking about?" She giggled at her own joke.

"Yeah, yeah, keep saying that," I took more of her popcorn, and her mouth dropped open when I did that. She put the bucket down and tackled me to the ground as we laughed at each other.

*****

She always encouraged me to tell Rocket about my feelings, but I'm still trying to figure everything out. At first, I thought it was weird thinking these things about him, but now I'm slowly getting comfortable with the fact that I *like him*. This crush has become harder to ignore since we came to Union Beria. I don't know why. This place makes me feel less bound to certain things than our realm. At home, people wish death upon others like myself and Moss, where others are blaming us for things that we had no control over and where a disease makes everyone afraid of you even if you don't have it. But in Union Beria, there is a sense of acceptance for some reason.

No one here is the same as the next. Everyone lives in peace and has the power to be free, at least before the invasion of Humans. Damn, Humans fucking suck.

Iris came out from the back door with a tray of cups and a teapot. "Tea is ready, my dears. It's an herbal mixture collected from the forest," Iris put the tray on a small table. She poured a cup for everyone, then sat in the chair across from me. "So, what brings you to this neck of the woods? We don't get many visitors."

"Well, we are on our way to help Union Beria by fighting against the Humans, Ma'am," Darwin answered.

"I see, and please, Iris is just fine. Calling me 'Ma'am' makes me feel older than I already am," the woman jokes. "But these are the saviors I've heard so much about through the grapevine. You all are so young. Why would they put the fate of the colonies in the hands of children? No offense."

"None taken because we would like to know the same thing, Iris," Wasma replied, taking a sip of tea, "This is amazing. Thank you."

"Of course! You are guests, after all, and as well as soon-to-be saviors," Iris paused for a second and sniffed the air, "Damnit! The bread! Excuse me, children." She ran inside, cursing under her breath.

As Iris ran inside, a tall Buckman, Ruby's father, approached the deck and took a cup from the tray. "Why, hello! Ruby, you didn't tell me you were having friends over," Ruby's dad said.

"What friends? Ruby doesn't have friends," Hudson replied, coming up behind his father.

"Eat shit, Hudson! Anyway, these are travelers, Papa. They helped Lilith, and to repay them for their kindness, I invited them for drinks and food, just like you taught me." Ruby looked up to her father.

"Watch your mouth, Rue, but I did teach you that, didn't I? Thank you, children, for helping our little Lilith out. She's been a cranky soul for a while now," the man spoke with a grin.

Right after he spoke, Iris yelled from inside the house. "OWEN! HELP! THE OVEN IS ON FIRE!"

"I'll be right back! I have to go save the day again," Ruby's dad, Owen, said as he ran into the house.

"Are you sure it's alright for us to be here? We don't want to bother you and your family," Clover asked Ruby.

"No, you guys are perfectly fine being here. This is just a normal day for us. It's expected for my mom to burn something at least once a week," she responded.

"I heard that, Ruben Lee Bashwin! " Iris's voice yelled out.

"And I'm always getting yelled at," Ruby chuckled. It wasn't a normal chuckle that you would hear when someone says something funny, though. It was more of a chuckle you give out when you try to hide that what was said or done upset you. It's pretty easy to pick up on when you do it yourself.

The woods were very peaceful. However, with a cup of tea, it was even better. We all sat outside, for what was probably hours, explaining to the Bashwin's about the journey we had been on as we tried to get to The Center. In return, Iris shared stories about their work in the Bewitched Forest.

It felt nice to take a real break from everything. Stopping at the TreeTrunk Motel wasn't technically a break; we didn't even get much sleep. Sitting here with everyone reminded me more of home—when Rocket and Moss's families came over for holiday dinners, and we'd relax all around each other like a real *family.* My friends, my father, and my friends' families are my family, and they always will be—forever and ever.

Turning my head to look at where Moss was sitting, I realized she wasn't next to me anymore. Now, thinking about it, I haven't seen her for an hour or two. I excused myself from the conversation to see if I could find her. She wasn't in the house or near the Floraloxy coop. I checked the front of the cabin, and she wasn't there either. I even checked in the forest, but still nothing. That's when Pascal, one of the twin brothers Ruby had, found me looking around.

"Can I help you with anything, uh..." Pascal asked me.

"Cricket. My name's Cricket, and yes. Have you seen my friend Moss? The one with the blond braids and the sunflower sweater?" I replied.

"Ah, well, Cricket, I think I saw her and Ruby walk to the pond. I can show you where to find it if you'd like?" Pascal suggested.

"That would be wonderful," I said, following him to the pond, where we peered behind what looked like a shed.

"So why are we watching over them? I thought you were looking for your friend?" Pascal questioned.

"Technically, yes, but now that I know where she is and who she's with, I'm not worried," I told the older boy.

"Are you talking about Ruby? She can't even hurt a fly, let alone a person," he mentioned.

"Good to know, actually,"

"Let me guess: You either like your friend or you're a wingman," Pascal looked at me.

"What?! No, gross, I don't like her in that way. She's like a sister to me. Anyway, we both like someone else," my voice filled with shock from Pascal's comment.

"So, you're the wingman, got it. She does look like the type to hate any man that looks at her weirdly," he observed.

"You have no idea," I looked back at Ruby and Moss.

The two of them were in a deep conversation. Moss was sitting a small distance away from her on a large rock. I watched as they talked; they inched closer to each other occasionally.

"Moss likes my sister, doesn't she?" Pascal asked me.

"...It isn't my right to tell you if so or not," I spoke clearly.

"Look, I get it. Would it help if I said that Ruby was a big ole woman lover?" He acknowledged.

"You mean a lesbian?"

"What the hell is a lesbian?" His eyebrows were stitched together.

"It's when a girl likes other girls and stuff like that," I explained.

"Then yeah, that's what she is," Pascal responded.

I went silent for a moment. I wanted Moss to be the one that told others about herself, not anyone else. She told me these things because she trusted me enough to do so. I guess Ruby has been out about this for a while now, which is something Moss and I could never do at home.

Pascal hit my shoulder and pointed to where Moss and Ruby were sitting. There wasn't any space between them, and their arms overlapped, which meant...

"Are they holding hands?" I looked up at Ruby's brother.

"It seems so," Pascal smirked lightly. He looked happy to see his little sister enjoying herself out there. "She's growing up too fast," he said.

"Growing up is painful, but it must be harder for siblings," I hinted.

"Yeah, it is..." He went silent and spoke again, " I hope you know if your little friend hurts my baby sister. I swear on the Tree Guardians—" he began to say.

"Moss isn't like that. She couldn't hurt a fly even if she wanted to," I patted Pascal's shoulder and walked away slowly back to the deck.

I turned my head slightly, now seeing Ruby's head gently lying on Moss's shoulder. I smile softly at the view. Moss means the world to me; if she's happy, then I'm happy for her. Regardless, she is the braver one out of the two of us.

Chapter 13
When Trees Fall, Do They Make A Sound?

*T*he sunlight moved from over the pond to the top of the trees. I think it might be the afternoon in Union Beria, as the suns were hot on my skin as they shined down on me directly. (Yes, *suns*, plural. This realm had two suns instead of one. I don't know how I didn't notice when we arrived here.) We must have spent hours with the Bashwin family. Their way of talking made me want to sit and listen to them for hours, maybe even days. I learned much about the colonies through the stories Owen and Iris told. Both Moxie and Neo came out at some point and joined the conversation.

"I can't believe you three came from a different realm just to help us. That's considerate, knowing that not many people would have come all this way to save people they didn't even know." Moxie held her baby brother in her arms. Her tone of voice was a mixture of flatness and maybe empathy. It was similar to Wasma's tone but more earthy.

"Well, we didn't know what was in store for us when we came here. We're still trying to put the pieces together," I said, lying back in the chair.

"[11]Да, да! Even here, it still feels like a dream. It doesn't feel real to me, yet I'm here living through it," Rocket commented.

During our discussion, Ruby and Moss ran back to the rest of us in a panic.

"Papa! Papa! The trees!" Ruby yelled, trying to get our attention.

Owen got out of his chair, as did the rest of us. We rushed down to Ruby and Moss and followed them.

"What's going on?" I asked.

"The decay is spreading," Robin, another brother of Ruby, answered.

"Decay?" Rocket's face lifted.

"Remember what the letter and Mrs. RedRoom said? They said the colonies have limited time left before it's all gone—before

---

[11] Да, да!: Yes, yes! (da, da)

it deteriorates entirely. I guess it has already spread to The Center," Darwin reminded.

"I didn't realize how close we were to that point," Clover added.

I saw MariGold put her leaf hand over her mouth in shock from the sight as the decaying area crept up the tree sides and over its leaves. The patch of woods we looked at was like a cemetery of dead trees. One after the other, they fell to the forest floor. Trees do make a sound when they fall; they scream and cry out in pain and agony. It felt as if the decaying was crawling towards us, like it was going to destroy us if it touched our bodies.

"Guys, we should get going," Wasma turned around, about to walk away.

"Wait! Is there anything we can do here?" Iris asked, grabbing her baby Neo from the ground and holding him tighter.

Wasma turned to the woman again. Her face had a different expression than usual. Her face was ridden with fear. "Mrs. Bashwin, I don't know. Like you said when we arrived, we're just children. We shouldn't have been given the job to save the whole fucking colonies!" Wasma's voice cracked. I could see the stress building in her body as her small neck tics became more noticeable. "I'm sorry, but we have no way of helping. I can only advise you to get as far away from here as possible. Get away from the decay and get yourselves and the Floraloxies to safety."

Darwin walked up to Wasma, hand on her shoulder, and whispered something to her. She took a deep breath, trying to self-soothe herself.

"I can speak for everyone here when I say thank you for everything today. We haven't had the time to relax in almost two days now," Darwin thanked the Bashwin's.

Iris nodded, "Of course, my dears. You go save our home from those monsters." She looked at her family. "Okay, boys, start gathering the birds. Moxie, get our emergency packs ready. Owen, find the tents for when we find a safe place to set up camp far from here. Let's go, let's go!" The Bashwin's ran to follow their orders. "Ruby! Help your sister and father."

Ruby peered at her family and us, then at Moss, "No."

"No?! Young lady, get your butt moving," Iris told her child.

"Where do you need to go? I know The Center like the back of my hand," Ruby ignored her mother's yells.

"We need to find the Towers of Unity," Clover said.

"Great! I know a way there that will make sure you guys won't be found or followed," Ruby walked in front of us as we stood still.

"Ruben Lee Bashwin! Get yourself back here now!" Iris yelled once again.

The fawn girl faced the group. "You came here to save Union Beria and said all help was needed, right? I don't want to stay and wait for a war to break out. Each person in my family has a role and job when coming to and giving back to our land. I don't. All I get when I do anything right or wrong is yelled at. Though I am not good at fighting, I'm sure as hell good at helping others. Now are we going to stand here, or are you guys going to kick some Human scum's ass?"

She seriously wanted in on our adventure. How could we say no?

"Alright, let's get going then," Darwin rolled his shoulders back. Ruby gave a brave grin as we all moved towards her, away from the cabin and the other deer people.

Moss grabbed Ruby's hand as we made our way through more trees and tall grass. We were so close to the end; I could feel it. We left Ruby's home as her mother still yelled her name, though Ruby walked away with her head high in front of danger. How? How can she leave everything behind without a single thought warning her? Wait, didn't I do the same thing?

Chapter 14
Towers Of Unity

*R*uby guided us through the forest. We took many turns trying to make sure we didn't walk into anything diseased by the decay, which was hard. The area we had to walk through was already hit by it, so we just had to be careful not to stand in the dead places for too long. My mind was filling up with millions and trillions of thoughts. When will the fight begin? When will this all be over with? Will we survive? Everything in my brain paused when I looked at everyone. They don't look as anxious as I am. Am I just overreacting to all of this? It feels like I'm the only one who cares that we will be in a fight in who knows how long. Like Moss said in the forest back home, I don't want to die out here. The biggest threat back home was coyotes and poison ivy, maybe, but here, people are hunting after us, wanting us dead and captured.

The suns made everything worse. It was like every summer day, times a hundred, and the trees weren't blocking any sunlight.

"We should be at the Towers of Unity soon. I'm putting all my bets on the table when I say that it is likely that soldiers will be stationed by and in the towers," Ruby turned her head to speak, her hand intertwined with Moss'.

While looking at their hands, a feeling crept into my chest. It was similar to the feeling I got in the woods while we were back home. Now, thinking about it, I realize this feeling wasn't like the normal jealousy I'd felt many times before. I was envious. Maybe I was always envious. They looked so happy, hand in hand, glued to the hip since Moss walked up to her. Why can't I feel that? The feeling of his hand in mine. I know that I'm to blame for these feelings. I refuse to talk to him just in case there is a sliver of a chance of him hating me after I tell him that I like him. Yeah, I am definitely envious. I envy Moss and Ruby's relationship and Moss and Rocket's, even if I know one of these relationships is only platonic.

I returned my attention to the group as we stopped by a large rock. "Why are we stopping?" I asked.

"We are on the border of entering the area where the towers are, and we have to make a plan to sneak in," Wasma replied, pointing at the open area between the trees.

My eyes instantly saw what she was pointing to. It looked dead. From what I could see, there were no people or creatures for miles except the Human soldiers. They held their weapons with such strength that it made me gulp down my spit.

"Humans don't look so friendly, no offense," Clover mentioned, looking over at Moss, Rocket, and I.

"You would be right. Most are not friendly," Rocket agreed with her.

"It's like they have no soul. How can people live that way forever? Why hold onto so much anger and hatred?" MariGold added.

"It's because these soldiers don't have hearts. If anything, they have black hearts and no mind of their own. Woah, Cricket, your mom would be an awesome soldier," Rocket smirked over at me, trying to lighten up the situation. I flipped him off in response. Though he was right, it wasn't the right timing, but I guess the best jokes are made at the worst times. He should know; he does it a lot.

"Can I please get all of your attention over here?" Acorn called our attention back to the rock where he stood, with the map spread out on top of it—the same map we used in the meeting building on Ascomycota Island.

Ruby pointed out places on the map, "Okay, there are three towers with many entrances. There are normally three to four, depending on the building you go in. Two are above-ground, rotating doors. But there are also underground ones too. People use those entrances when they don't want to go up all the stairs to enter their workplace." Ruby explained.

"They are also there because of the tube system. Everyone in Union Beria uses these tubes for transportation. Anyway, there are halls that you can enter that bring you inside the towers. " Acorn said.

The tubes they spoke of reminded me of the subway in New York City, where you can be transported to work without much effort.

"I think we should go through the tube entryway instead of the above grounds," Acorn concluded.

Darwin had his hand on his chin, looking at the map. "Sounds good enough for me. Don't think our tube cards can work for this."

"I wouldn't put it past the Humans to keep an eye out for any sign of us," Wasma said.

After a bit of finalizing the plan, it was perfect! Wasma was able to conjure up some items to cover ourselves with. (The girls were given a headscarf, as we guys got hats.) Darwin removed his hoodie from across his chest and put it on, pulling the hood over his head and the hat. Rocket and Acorn tied their hair up and stuffed it into their hats. The girls used the fabrics to cover most of their hair and portions of their faces. I had to say, MariGold was the one that pulled it off the best. How she wore it reminded me of how some women wore a hijab.

When all was done, we made our way out of the forest into the open area. Just like how it looked in the Bewitched Forest, the town (if you could even call it that) looked so dreadful. Other than the soldiers, the only people around were coming in and out of shops or small places of work. As soon as we started walking, a bell rang. We looked at each other, confused. That's when everyone and their mother came rushing out of every establishment, speed walking to the underground transportation or to other buildings. It was as if it was rush hour in the city.

"I don't think we will be able to stay with each other very long," Moss mentioned.

"New plan! Darwin, Rocket, and Cricket, you go to the third building. Moss, Ruby, MariGold, and Acorn go to the first building. Clover, Peep, and I will go into the second. It will make things easy for us instead of going as a group to each one!" Wasma yelled to us over the loud crowd.

"How will we meet up again?" Clover asked, holding Peep tight in her arms.

"The Walkie-Talkies!" I remembered as I searched my bag.

"Shit, almost forgot about the metal bricks," Moss grabbed her string bag, shoving items out of the way. "Here! I was holding onto mine, and Rocket's just in case we needed them."

"What's a 'Walkie-Talkie'?" Darwin's eyes squinted.

"A communication device. Wasma, have Rocket's for the time being. Just push this button on the side here and speak into the microphone. We will be able to talk to you through it. After you're done talking, take your fingers off the button and wait for a reply," I showed Wasma what to do.

I gave her the Walkie-Talkie, and we split into the three groups, entering the underground tube entryway. Not soon after we lost sight of the others, we were surrounded by what seemed to be hundreds of people and creatures.

Darwin grabbed Rocket's wrist as he pulled us to the third building's underground hall entrance. Rocket then grabbed my hand—not my wrist, not my arm—*my hand*—and pulled me behind them both. His hand was warm, and the tips of his fingers were rough. I wasn't all that surprised by this. To be honest, this boy is a walking and talking heater and plays his guitar almost every day back home without a guitar pick.

The three of us scrambled up the massive flight of stairs. As we did so, Rocket commented that he was never wearing skinny jeans again.

There had to be at least two hundred stairs because my legs wanted to crumble in on themselves once we reached the top. We had made it to the checkpoint for card checks and carefully jumped over them. I was surprised that the soldiers weren't scanning for us. If they were, then they fucking sucked at it. Anyway, we got to a rotating door and entered them with ease.

Now inside, I stopped in my tracks in awe. The building looked more humongous from the inside than it looked from the outside. The floors were made of bright white porcelain. Every step I took frightened me as if I'd crack the floor in one single step. The ceiling was painted with images of (what I understood) the Elder Tree Guardians, Goddesses, Fairyians, Floralins, Gnomians, Trollians, Witches, Warlocks, Sirens, Mushians and so much more. The details were so small and precise that it must have taken thousands of years to paint. Twelve columns were holding the different levels within the tower. In the center of the room was a large spiral staircase that went up to the top floor and had little platforms when reaching each new level. My brain couldn't fully comprehend how gorgeous the interior was. It reminds me of what people have said about how Olympus would look in real life.

Rocket and I followed Darwin to the stairs and went up them. I wish this journey didn't involve so many staircases in such a short time. I was so distracted by the colors of the beautiful mural that I didn't even feel that Rocket's hand was still in mine. He squeezed my hand in a pulse-like pattern. My face started to burn up from the feeling. I tried to snap out of it (for the millionth time) when Rocket questioned something.

"What do we do now?" Rocket asked Darwin.

I hadn't given much thought to that question. I was just doing what everyone else was doing and didn't even question why we were here. "Yeah, exactly what are we doing in the Towers of Unity?" I re-stated Rocket's query.

"The letter said, *'Once you arrive, the One will find what is awaiting for Him.'*" Darwin took a second to think.

"What do they mean by 'Him'?" I stared at the Warlocks back with a puzzled look.

"I've got no clue. The Elders could mean we will be meeting another Tree Guardian. I don't know, but we must see and find out, right? If anything, there is a one-in-three chance we will find the answer; the others could have better odds of understanding it. I suppose we just walk around till something calls out for us," he shrugged.

Great, the best news to get is always *'wait and see what happens.'* (I'm being sarcastic if you can't tell.) I've always hated moments like this, positive or negative. Why not tell us what we are looking for? I don't want to decipher a letter made by technically supernatural trees born millions of years ago. If they wanted this to be easy, they would have just told us what we had to find, more precisely who, if that's what the letter meant. Maybe it's a metaphor? The *'Him'* and *'One'* could mean... no, it wouldn't make sense in that way. I continue to rack my brain around who or what the 'Him' and 'One' were.

We had stopped at the forty-eighth floor, thinking the Elders would put some sympathy on us and not make us go to the top. Anyway, the sign for the floor said *'History Museum'*, and we also hoped that would help us a little. Once there, Darwin suggested that we should check the areas separately. He suggested he'd go to the right hallway, and Rocket and I would go to the left. After he said his idea, he gave me a slight wink.

"What if a Human spots you? You don't have a Walkie-Talkie," Rocket spoke, no longer holding my hand. It felt cold not having his warm hand in mine.

"This place is extremely echoey. If something happens, we can just yell for each other. Once we finish our sweep through, we'd meet at the stairs and repeat on the other levels, if necessary." Darwin spoke like a true leader.

"Okay then, I guess we'll see you in a bit," I gave him a weak smile.

Rocket and I turned to walk to the left hallway when I twisted my head to see Darwin giving me a thumbs-up. Even in a dangerous time, he was wishing me luck. Oh God, Gods, Tree Guardians, whoever will listen, please send help.

Chapter 15
Shaking Statues

Statues, that was what this hallway was full of. Every time I see one, it brightens my heart a bit. There is so much history in such a large lump of marble. Even in their lifeless eyes, you know the stories, the hardships, and the endings that brought them to where they are now.

I stare at the marble lumps for a long time, admiring the cuts and creases that make them come to life. Though I don't know most of these Goddesses and Tree Beings, I feel equal to them here. My eyes wander to a statue in the center of the room. The white marble shone brightly in the double sun's light pouring in from a window. I stopped in front of it, looked down at the metal engraved plate, and read it:

"Two Lovers,
   With Love, there is Light,
   With Light, there is Darkness.
   Come forth to not live in the shadows,

Come forth and Love One Another.
Love cannot be hidden."
        –Two Lovers"

"Beautiful, isn't it?" Rocket stood next to me.

I hadn't realized he stood by my side. "Damn it, Keith! Stop doing that!" I jumped from hearing his voice.

"Sorry, Cherry," Rocket smirked.

"I told you to stop calling me that," I looked back at the statues.

"Do you think it's a man and a woman?" Rocket asked me, ignoring my comment.

When looking hard at the statues, I couldn't tell. It was of two people kissing. Both were covered, and both had long hair. That still doesn't say much of anything. It is common for people in general to have long hair here and back at home. It was the '80s, so it makes sense. So no, I couldn't tell if it was a man with a woman, a man with a man, or a woman with a woman.

"I suppose it's up to interpretation," I replied, eyes still transfixed on the two lovers.

"I think it is of a man and a man. It would make it worth more to me that way." Rocket said quietly. Before I could add anything to the conversation, Rocket strolled away. Something had caught his eye. "Cricket, is this Adrastus?" Rocket spun his head.

I left the Two Lovers Statue and came to where he was. "You're right, it is Adrastus. He was the king of Argos. Why do they have Greek statues here?" My face scrunched up.

"No clue," Rocket looked down at the metal plate and read it. *"King Adrastus of Argos, home from the Ancient Greek world, from the realm of Humans. He was said to have made the first temple for the Goddess Nemesis, Goddess of Revenge. Adrastus symbolizes the inescapable."*

Every word Rocket spoke hung from my ears, mainly just one, *inescapable*. "Eh, look at this! *'Written by Albuh Pakín'* I know that name," Rocket looked at me.

My eyes were still on the statue, hypnotized by it. It took a few moments for me to answer Rocket. "Oh yeah, that's Darwin's last name. He said his father was a geographer and studied ruins in his free time. Maybe he, I don't know, mentioned Greek mythology to the Guardians, and they were interested? Who knows."

"Cool," Rocket walked away again, leaving me in front of the sculpture of Adrastus.

I don't know why I am fixed on him. There is no reason I should. But there was this gut feeling, this intuition to get closer. I couldn't control my legs from moving, my arm raising, and my hand gently caressing his cold marble hand.

I don't know what being struck by lightning feels like, but a sharp pain entered my body. I felt the pain shoot from the top of my head to the bottom of my spine with a force unlike anything I've experienced, causing my body to stiffen. Hitting my back and head on the porcelain floor caused me to yell. I felt like I was going to die from the pain.

After I fell on the floor, a huge vibration, like an earthquake, started. The vibrations were intense and persistent. The pottery began to fall, and the sculptures shook. I shut my eyes tight, in too much pain to move, as I saw Adrastus start to tilt toward me. I felt two arms grab me and push me away from the spot I was once in. Rocket had dived in so I didn't get smashed by a statue that weighed more than he and I combined.

"Rocket—augh! What's happening?!" My jaw was tight, and it took everything out of me not to cry. The sounds of marble crashing continued.

"I don't know, but I'm not sticking around to find out!" Rocket replied. "Darwin! Darwin!" He began yelling. He helped me up, trying to get to the stairs, but they were too crowded with people fleeing in fear.

I saw Darwin run over to us from the other side of the building. "What the hell is going on?" Darwin yelled, trying to stay steady.

Rocket began to reply when I screamed. "What?!" Rocket looked at me with worry as I pointed at the floor. The porcelain was cracking.

"We need to get out of here now!" Rocket panicked and moved away from the cracks.

"How can we get out of here? We are on the forty-eighth floor!" Darwin was panicking, too.

"I have an idea." Rocket said. He closed his eyes as his midnight black wings stretched out from his back. While he did so, his face was contorted with a painful look.

"Rocket, don't you dare. It is too dangerous to get out of here with you flying–" Darwin was starting to say as Rocket grabbed onto both of us tightly.

"Well, I guess we have to see what happens then!" Rocket began to run straight for the windows.

"Keith! What the *fu*-!" I yelled at him.

Not even seconds later, we were smashing through a window, falling. I was waiting for the moment that we would hit the ground and die. I waited and waited, but nothing happened. We were floating down slowly in the air.

"Holy shit, it worked!" Rocket laughed.

"I hate you so much right now! We could have died if it didn't work!" Darwin reprimanded him.

"Hey, we are alive. I told you we would be fine," he rolled his eyes.

Sooner or later, we landed on the ground. I won't say it was a great landing, but it was good enough for his first time flying. I sat up, looking at the hundreds of people and creatures running away from the three towers in panic. Windows had broken, and floors came crashing, but the building stood straight up. I stared at it, confused as ever.

My ears perked up as someone yelled our names.

"Cricket! Rocket! Oh my God, are you guys, okay?!" Moss ran over to us while the rest of the group followed behind her. Though out of breath, she hugged all three of us tightly when she reached us. I patted her head, telling her we were fine. After Moss let us go, she started bombarding us with questions, asking what happened, if we were hurt, and everything.

"I'm not sure. I was just looking at a statue. I touched it, and then I felt this shooting pain go through me, making me collapse, and that's when the shaking started," I explained.

"What do you mean shooting pain?" Acorn asked.

"The pain felt as if I was hit with a high volt of vibrations all happening at once. I could feel my spine shake."

"My Tree Guardian, you set off the violent earthquake," Wasma looked at me. "I guess we didn't need those talky thingies after all."

I looked at her, confused, "How did *I* set them off?"

"Aren't your powers one with a cricket?" Acorn questioned, tilting his head, waiting for the answer.

"Yes?"

"From what I've read, crickets can set off low vibrations. Usually, they do it when they're doing their mate calling. But when there is a threat, they use more aggressive vibrations to tell the predator to back off. I think what you just experienced was you receiving the rest of your powers." Acorn sounded so happy to tell me about crickets. Why was he reading books about crickets? Did he run out of things to do? The world will never know.

Darwin faced me, "You are the *'Him'* in question; *'Once you arrive, the One will find what is awaiting for Him.'* You found what you needed, which was the rest of your powers."

I shifted in my place. Just by getting my powers, I damaged a whole building and could have hurt or killed people inside. Can this get any worse?

MariGold tried to speak, but everyone else was talking over her. "Guys, hey guys?" She cleared her stem throat and yelled over us, "*PEOPLE!*" We became quiet at once after she yelled. I don't think she has ever spoken over much of a whisper before, so it was surprising.

"Thank you," MariGold said, back in her normal voice. "I think we should *really* leave."

"Why?" Clover asked her.

"*Because* a huge group of Humans are quickly coming over here," MariGold spoke through her teeth, pointing at the Humans with her leaf hands.

"Why didn't you just start with that?!" Clover replied.

"I tried! You all were talking over me!" The Floralin gave a dumbfounded look to the Fairyian.

"Oh, I'm sorry, darlin'. But yes, we should listen to her and get the hell out of here," Clover turned to the rest of us.

We didn't want to wait any longer than needed because once we started to move away from the area we were in, the Human soldiers began to run after us. Great, another chasing game. I spoke too soon about what could get worse. I need to learn to zip my mouth shut. At this point, I'm just going to jinx it.

Soldiers chased us down from all directions, yelling at us to stop running. As they yelled more and more, I saw Rocket flip them off and almost trip on a root. I would have laughed at him if we weren't fleeing for our lives. We ran through a small patch of trees, and it felt like they were trying to grab us with its branches. We entered an open field after getting out of the trees, but it only worsened. A line of soldiers stood on the other side with their weapons facing us.

"Well fuck. We have nowhere to go," Wasma cursed, stopping in her tracks like the rest of us did.

All ten of us were in the center of the field, with the only exits being guarded by angry soldiers and an open ocean on the other. My breath was trying to catch up with my heart. We were totally screwed to every level of life.

Chapter 16
You Called?

*W*e stopped short in our tracks. The soldiers grouped in a circle around us, armed and waiting.

"You can't run anymore. Let's get you all back to the South Wing to talk. I don't think any of you want a fight, right?" One of the men spoke out. I assume he was some form of lieutenant, as his uniform was similar to what Father used to wear.

"Hell no. We are not going anywhere," Wasma told the Lieutenant.

He sucked at his teeth, "Ah, Wasma. We have been looking for you and your friend, but I think you knew we were."

Wasma gave the man a death glare that made the hair on my neck stand.

"Why do you have to make this harder for everyone here? You gotta be kidding me. Why can't you colonizers piss off? Haven't you guys taken enough? They just want to be left alone and live in peace, you shitheads!" Moss shouted towards the men.

"None of you get it, do you? We are here for *it*,"

"What do you mean by 'it'?" Moss asked.

"The magic, how this place came into existence. With this amount of power, our world will become powerful, and we could expand our life force further than our simple dying Earth," the Lieutenant explained.

"That's not how it works, and you know it. Everyone in the South Wing has told you that from the beginning. You have to get it through your thick skulls. We can't give you the power to do that. You have to be gifted it from birth." Wasma stepped closer as she spoke but was replied to with guns raised at her. Moss grabbed her shoulder and pulled her back as Darwin and Rocket stepped in front of her.

"Aw, how adorable. The Warlock is trying to protect his friends, and so is the Human boy. Do you think we are scared to kill some kids?" The man gave a small chuckle. "Do you know how many we have killed to get here?

Fairies, flower people, gnomes, Witches, Warlocks, Tree Beings. Nothing will stop us from getting that power. Not even the kids those tree bastards put in charge to 'save the world.' Absolutely pathetic."

"Pathetic?! What *we*- No, *you* Humans are doing is pathetic. You can't gain power, so you steal it from others!" Anger filled my body. It is not pathetic to protect your home. They have been harming others for generations and get away with it every time, and they dare to call it pathetic.

"Enough! Your time has expired to speak. You only have two options, kids. You can surrender to us, or we fight," the Lieutenant stood straighter in his place. He probably thinks we are going to give up just like that. Now that's pathetic.

I turned to Darwin, "We can't just raise our white flag."

"I wasn't planning on leaving without a fight," Darwin's eyes met mine as he placed a big smirk on his face. "But we might need some backup, of course."

I looked at him, confused, and then it clicked. "Don't we have a favor to call in? She did try to kill us after all," I returned the smile.

"How could I forget her? Wasma, do you remember how to do a *siren summoning call?*" The Warlock boy faced the soldiers as he spoke, showing we won't back down.

"Of course I do," Wasma said, grabbing something from her knapsack and raising it into the sky. In her pale hands, she held a set of pearl-like bells.

She began to shake them, sending out a loud ring with each movement. The water from the ocean started to rise, and waves crashed viciously on the land's edge. That's when Cyrus appeared. Her scaly tail morphed into two tan legs and created a scaled skirt to cover her bottom half as she stepped out of the water. Her hands moved through her hair as the rest of her body turned to the tan color of her now legs. The pearled top she had stayed the same—the same exposed chest covered by the pearled chains. The more she moved her hair, it began to change. Her hair started to stretch out towards her back, creating bird-like wings. After all, they didn't call her the Ancient Siren for nothing.

"You called? 'Cause I've been waiting for you too," Cyrus' voice was more evident than when we were in the tube. Her Australian-like accent could catch even the smallest of insects' attention.

"Would you like to join us? I believe you have a taste for Humans, right?" Darwin asked Cyrus.

"My favorite treat," Cyrus grinned with an evil smile, her tongue gliding over her sharp shark teeth.

"The Siren!" A soldier yelled, all facing their guns and weapons directly at her.

"Oh, you make it no fun when you use weapons," Cyrus used a mocking sad voice and laughed. Her laugh ended abruptly as she made a loud, ear-piercing whistle. Once she did, splashes from the water came about as other Sirens rose to the land, their tails whipping around.

I looked from the Sirens back to the Humans. One soldier was whispering into the Lieutenant's ear. I closed my eyes, hoping to amplify my hearing like I did in the forest.

"Sir, the Sirens here make this a larger threat. We should begin the attack," the soldier whispered.

I leaned into Darwin's ear, "They're going to attack, so be ready, okay?"

"I'm as ready as I'll ever be," Darwin replied.

The Lieutenant raised his weapon, yelling to attack, and just like that, with only one word, the fight had started. Humans versus a Fairyian, a Floralin, a Gnomian, a Trollian, a Warlock, a Witch, a Fawn, a dozen Sirens, an Ancient Siren, and three Pures.

Darwin Pakún

PART TWO

Chapter 17
Beacon Of The Shadows

*W*eapons rose as they charged at us: knives, guns, and any essential weapon that would be used in combat, they had.

Could you compare magic and weaponry on the same level? I suppose it would depend on how you define *'magic.'* When you have the shadows of destruction inside your mind and body, I think that would give you the high ground.

From all sides of me, my friends, yes, my *friends*, charged right at the soldiers without fear in their hearts. The shouting of my friends entered my ears, but even with their voices blaring on my eardrums, I could hear the voice. It beckoned to me, pleading my name over and over again.

"...Darwin..."

"...Darwin..."

All I could do was stand in the middle of the field while everyone else was fighting. I was frozen in place; my vision started to go black, the voice getting louder.

"Darwin, it is time," the Human Shadow spoke.

Once again, my body got heavy and dropped to the ground, but this time, I dropped to my knees, and my head hung back towards the sky. Everything was black, and then I was sitting in the same old uncomfortable chair in the waiting room—the same ugly striped-colored waiting room with the same stale smell that filled it.

Like always, my legs automatically stood up and walked through the doors that swayed open even when there was no breeze to do that.

"Let me guess, it's time?" I spoke out to the dark void.

"How did you guess?" The Human Shadow replied, but its voice sounded deeper as if there was more than one thing talking at a time.

"I got a hunch when you kept repeating my name over and over again like a fucking maniac!" My tone was getting gradually louder.

"No need to shout. We can hear you just fine,"

"Who's we?"

"The shadows of the void, you know that very well by now,"

I fidget with my sweatshirt, "I've been thinking, what if I don't want to do this anymore? Have you ever thought about what I wanted out of this?"

"Darwin, we all know you have little to no decision-making in this divine plan. You will let us enter the Mainland whether you like it or not!"

"Don't you threaten me. I will make sure you don't ever see the light of Union Beria if you keep making open-ended threats,"

"Oh? Well, what about your 'friends'? Are you going to leave them to fight and get killed by those nasty Human-scum? We both know you can't leave the void willingly. I also know that you don't wish to leave your friends in danger," the Human Shadow gave an evil chuckle at the end. "And we both know my threats are never 'open-ended.' They just get put to the side for a better time, for a better use."

I look around the darkness. Nothing I can do wouldn't risk the others' safety.

"If I let you leave, you must promise me that you and all the other shadows will behave yourselves. And that they will not touch my friends, not any of them. Swear it on the Elder Trees' lives that you will not harm anyone other than the Human Soldiers,"

"We swear our promise,"

"Fine..." I took a deep breath, "You may use me as your beacon to enter Union Beria," I looked at my feet.

"Our time has come!" Spoke all the shadows of the void.

I could feel how they came spewing out of me onto the battlefield. The shadows crawled through my throat, ready to start their mischief. The Human Shadow and its counterparts lunged at soldiers, throwing and toying with them, even some of the shadows possessing them.

Looking to my left and right, everyone looked at me confused, except Wasma, who had seen some of this before.

"Guys, come on! Just try to stay out of the shadows way!" Wasma yelled at the group, then returned to the fight.

Peep was the first to show its claws to the crowd. The ground around it began to pull together as Peep grew in size. It took dirt, rock, and moss into its body, and that's when it made an earthly growl. I remember how Peep looked in the forest minutes after it killed those soldiers. What I witnessed Peep do— if I was able to throw up, I wouldn't be able to stop. The brown dirt was now turning rich crimson. I've never seen so much blood and gore before in my life, and I think this image will not ever leave my mind for the rest of my life.

Wasma was flinging potions on the soldier's faces, burning their eyes, and then smashing the bottles on their heads. MariGold made the roots of plants come out of the ground and lifted the men in the air, making them drop their weapons, while Clover was in the air with her bow and arrows, hitting as many Humans as she could. She would also pick one or two men up into the sky and toss them into the water, where the Sirens would finish the job. Acorn swung his ax at the enemy, trying to keep Ruby safe. (Moss's orders, of course. She was there for help and support. We had to protect her with our lives.) Rocket started kicking the crap out of one of the soldiers, and once they were down on the ground, he grabbed him by the collar and threw the man into another one, then continued doing such with others. I could tell he was a fighter back in LongEdge for sure.

Moss grew her sunflowers from the ground, and the stems slithered around the soldiers' bodies and necks. To be honest, to witness her rage makes me fear the girl. I've never seen her or any of the others this angry in our time together over these past couple of days.

My body had given up on trying to move even an inch. I could feel myself becoming weaker as the shadows slashed at the evil men. From what I knew about the Human Shadow, we share the same energy source, but now that there are many more shadows than I'm used to, I don't even have enough energy to sit up straight. I keep reminding myself that I was born to be a beacon for all the void's shadows to use, and this is it.

The Human Shadow is dangerous, without order. It will attack whoever it wants to. To be quite frank, the Human Shadow scares everything out of me. Being here and not in control over any part of the situation makes me feel like a scared child. I am in pain, I am tired, and I just want this to be over already. Oh, Tree Guardians, please have mercy on me. I'm just so tired of this.

A tear ran from my eye. Wait, no, it wasn't. It was cold, but it didn't drip. More shadows were seeping out of my eyes. The shadow tears spread across my eyes till they turned black with wispy air.

All I could think was that I could not fully see and that this would last millions of years. I wish I were with my mom; I wish she could hold me tight and tell me everything was a horrible dream. That I wasn't limp on my knees while hundreds of shadows used me. I wish she could tell me that I wasn't meant to be just a beacon forever. I can't control them. It took so long just to learn teamwork with the Human Shadow. Why did I have to be born with a horrible prophecy, and why did it ever have to come true?

Maybe it was my delusional state from the energy being taken out of my body, but I swore that I heard my mother's voice speaking such kind words to me.

"My sweet boy, it will all be okay. You just need to live through this for a bit longer, and you can rest for a long time. I would know, I am your mother, and I know when my boy will make it out of anything

hard· Just keep fighting, baby," I heard my mom's voice speak to me.

"*M-mommy?*" I try to speak, but my mouth feels locked open and dry.

"*Hush, my boy· I am right here with you· Do not try to speak; it will only hurt more·*"

I could see my mom's face appear in the wispy black tears falling out of my eyes. She looks healthier in my mind than she does in real life. Her cheekbones weren't too sharp from sickness, and her eyes looked lively. I missed it when she looked like that. Mom can't even push her wheelchair anymore and is getting weaker by the day. I know I'm going to lose her one day, but I don't want that to happen. Not without me being by her side.

She put a hand on my face, and I swear I could feel it even if I knew she was not really there. She began to whisper to me in Treen, and of course, I didn't understand. It was rare for anyone who wasn't a Fairyian or Tree Guardian to understand and speak Treen, but my mom has spent her whole life learning it to tell prophecies to others who only knew Treen.

My mom, at least when I was very young, would sing and whisper to me in Treen, hoping I'd pick it up one day. Sadly, I didn't, but it never stopped her from yelling at me about my grades in it. Those memories are genuinely my favorite.

*****

"Mom, I'm home from school!" I yelled, walking into the house and putting my bag on the coat hook.

My mom was in the kitchen cooking something that made my nose happy. (This was at the beginning of my mom's illness, where she still had the strength and energy to stand.)

"What are you cooking? It smells amazing," I smile as I walk up to hug her, but she stops me from doing so with her hand. "What?" My eyebrows raise.

"Darwin, what did I tell you about your grades?" She put her hand down, grabbed a piece of paper from the counter, and gave it to me.

"I don't know what you mean. I get all A's and B's in my potion and magic classes."

"And a D in Treen class!" That's when she started to argue with me in Treen.

"Mama, you know I can't understand you or anything in that class. I've been telling you it just doesn't click."

"Save it, mister. By the end of the year, I want this grade to be at least a C+ or a B-."

"Can't you cut me a bit of slack, Mommy? I promise you I am trying," I put my head on her shoulder.

"I know you are, my dear, and I know things are getting hard in school and at home now, but I need you to try. If anything, try for me?" She laid her head on mine.

"I will, Mom, I promise with my whole heart." I went silent for a second, "Are you feeling any better today?"

My mom sighed and mumbled something I couldn't understand. *"No, not yet. But I'm telling you, I will get better! I can feel it."*

"You better," I looked at my mom from the side of my eyes. Her head was covered in a silk scarf tied off by the base of her neck. Her hair had started to thin for the past couple of weeks, and she refused to be around anyone without a scarf over her scalp. I kept telling her she didn't need to hide herself from me, but she never listened.

"Why aren't you wearing that new scarf Wasma gave you?" I asked her.

"Oh, I didn't think it matched my outfit," Mom replied with a simple smile.

"I think it would be lovely. I'll go fetch it," I told my mom as I dipped my finger into the curry-looking dinner, running away before she could hit me with her hand. She yelled my name but couldn't help but laugh at me.

I returned to the kitchen with the dark blue scarf that had star patterns all over it. Untying the one on her head already, I saw that Mom had lost more hair today. She gets ashamed of it so easily when it is nothing to be ashamed of.

I gently fixed the placing of the new silk scarf on Mom's head and tied it off. I grabbed her shoulders gently to turn her around to face me. I smiled brightly at her. "I told you, Mommy, it looks lovely with your outfit. You look like a queen," I tried so hard to keep the waterworks from showing, but when my mom started to cry, I couldn't help myself.

I held her tight in my arms and kissed the top of her head as we cried. We forgot about everything around us, even the dinner on the stove. It was just me and her forever, and it always will be.

*****

Cricket Mont

PART THREE

Chapter 18
Please Don't Leave

The shadows caused much destruction in the field. Soldiers were being thrown and pushed around everywhere. They tried shooting at it, but the darkness of the shadows just absorbed the blow. When the shadows attacked, it gave the rest of us the time to catch them distracted.

I never thought I'd have a fighter in me, but after a few good punches in these soldiers' faces, my knuckles were starting to bruise in the way that I smiled when looking down at them. I tried my best when using my vibrations to be set on specific areas, which came to me like riding a bike. All I had to do was focus my energy on my hands or feet and then hit it on the ground or a person. It would make them fly backward or trip over their own feet, but in any circumstance, they always landed on their asses. It was similar to the screeching in which the Sirens used to push and pull the Humans like rag dolls. Yes, the screeching affected us, but after a bit, it just became background noise.

I'm unsure when it happened, but the shadows coming from Darwin set off a vast dirt cloud that hazed my sight. It reminded me of when I'd kick up dry dirt as a kid, but this was a hundred times worse. Then, there was a yell from one of the girls.

"I can't see anyone! Is everyone alright?" I shouted.

Coughing from the distance was MariGold, "We're over here!" I ran over to her, by hearing alone, trying not to trip over the roots she had made during the fight.

Once I got to the others, I saw Wasma holding Clover's hand as Acorn and Ruby helped clean her eye wound. She cried out in more pain, holding onto Wasma's hand for dear life. She must have been hit by something during the fight. "Wasma, everything hurts!" Clover cried out to her, her cheeks covered with tears and blood.

Wasma grabbed her hand tighter, bringing it to her lips and kissing her hand. "I know, but we need to get the area cleaned so it doesn't get infected." She spoke softly to her. Ruby then tied a piece of cloth that MariGold tore off from her dress over the Fairyian's injured eye.

Clover tried to calm down, though still in extreme pain, when I saw something switch in her. "Where's Peep?" The air felt so thick after she spoke, "Peep? Peep?! Where are you?!" Clover used her hands to get up from the ground. We tried to stop her, telling her she needed to rest, but nothing worked. She kept calling out for Peep, but nothing came from it. I watched her as she tried to flutter her wings even though they were ripped. Still, she pushed herself to fly.

We knew when Clover found Peep. Clover's screams were blood-curdling as she fell to the ground. We all rushed to where she was to see her holding Peep in her arms. "Peep, please, please don't. No, no, no! Don't leave me like this! Peep, please wake up!" Her screams told us precisely what was happening. Peep was limp in her arms, *dead.*

"Clover..." Wasma kneeled next to her, "Clover, Peep's gone..."

"No! It can't be. Peep can't die, it just can't-" Clover tried to bargain, but Wasma interrupted her.

"Clover," Wasma looked straight at her face, both making eye contact. That moment, Clover looked from Wasma to Peep and held it tighter. She put her face into Wasma's chest and bawled her eyes out once again.

We stood there for what felt like forever, shedding tears with Clover as she mourned.

Even if we only knew Peep briefly, it was always there for us, protecting us. Other than the gunshots heard from behind us on the battlefield, Clover's cries could be heard over all of it. "You monsters! They get off on the death of others!"

I could feel the anger that radiated from her body. I recognized this type of anger too well. The kind that flows in your blood and makes it boil. She gently put Peep on the ground and got up. "I need my bow."

"Your bow snapped in half, Clover. It's broken," Ruby reminded her.

"Then give me your ax, Acorn," Clover replied. Acorn didn't want to argue with the enraged Fairyian and gave her what she wanted.

"Clove, you aren't in the right headspace to go fight. You need to rest," MariGold spoke up.

Clover stopped in her tracks, looking over at MariGold, "They killed my best friend, Mari. They are probably the same people that killed my dad. I'm not letting them harm anyone else I care about. I can't let them."

"Clover, I know you want them to suffer for what they have done, but you're going to hurt yourself more if you go back out there.

Peep wouldn't want you to get hurt any more than you already have," Marigold told her.

I watched as the Fairyian looked down at Peep's body lying cold in the dirt, tears growing again in her eyes.

Wasma grabbed Clover's arm. "You should stay with it. I think Peep would want to know that you were with it for its last moments."

Clover replied with a sigh, dropping the ax on the ground and falling to her knees.

"The fight seems to be kicking up again. We should go back," I whispered to Wasma.

"No, you and Ruby should stay here with Clover. She needs people to lean on," Wasma replied as the soldiers' yells started again. She knelt next to Clover and kissed the top of her head. "I promise to make it back to you, okay?"

Clover didn't reply, simply nodding, as Wasma got up and ran back to the field with MariGold and Acorn.

I sat beside her on the ground as Ruby did the same. The only thing keeping Clover sitting upright were her arms. Sniffles and tiny cries were the only noises she let out. She sat there in the dirt, numb, as she continued to look over Peep's body.

I looked over at the field as my friends fought. I wish I could have been out there to help, but right now, if we weren't with Clover, she would probably commit a mass murder on the Humans. None of us expected to be in a fight when we went into the forest that night, and likely, the others didn't think they would be doing this months ago. No one could have prepared us for something this gruesome and horrific. This wasn't something teens go through, maybe mental wars, but not physical ones. It wasn't normal, not even for a place like Union Beria. Wars shouldn't be normal. Trying to take over lands that aren't yours isn't normal. None of this is normal.

A thought ran through my mind. I wondered what Mama would think of me now. Moments ago, I was beating the life out of grown men. I no longer feel like the boy who needed his friends to fight his battles or a little boy that his mother could hit around. I am the guy who happened to be a Pure and was fighting for people I've read about in legends and stories. We, a group of teenagers, will win, and the soldiers, a group of adults, will lose. They will lose against a group of teenagers. I don't know how many people can say that, but I can. My chest, though filled with sadness from the loss of a friend, but also filled with pride in the fact that we will finish this war, and we *will* win.

The ground under where I sat caught me off guard. It began to move and shake, almost like the land was consuming itself. I stood up quickly, as did Ruby and Clover. The shaking was getting stronger. It differed from the vibrations I set off in the Towers of Unity; it was as if whatever was inside the ground was alive.

"What's going on?" I asked, watching the ground where Peep laid starting to engulf the Trollian, taking its body into the dirt.

"Oh, Tree Guardians, please- I'm not ready for Peep to leave yet!" Clover yelled to the ground, clawing at the dirt for Peep. When she was unsuccessful in grabbing it, she hit her hand over the warm dirt.

As quickly as Peep was there, it was gone. Clover continued to yell and curse at the spot where Peep once laid.

The ground started to shake vigorously now as something tried to crawl up to the surface. It was roots at first, then the roots formed a hand. I grabbed Clover's shoulder as all three of us backed up. Next was a long arm, which pulled a long torso out from the soil. This happened in minutes, maybe even seconds.

My eyes widened in terror, "What the hell is that?!"

"It's—" Ruby watched it come fully out of the ground. "It's a Tree Guardian?"

"No, it can't be. Peep was right there," Clover continued to bargain.

"*The day when we are reborn from the dirt, rock, and moss. A cycle that follows us forever till we are put to rest once again back to dirt, rock, and moss,*" Ruby recalled a saying, "It is one of the most known mottos in the colonies."

"Peep? Is that you?" Clover called out to the Tree Being.

The wooden creature looked down at us, his body still covered with dirt and moss. "*Iviny.* Sadly, Peep is no longer here. Peep is just a memory of mine before my rebirth. Iviny is my proper name," the Tree Being that once was Peep spoke.

"I can't believe it. I never realized that the saying was about Trollians and Tree Guardians," Ruby mentioned.

"Many never do..." Iviny said, looking up at the commotion. "Get off the field, all of you, and hide. I can continue from here."

None of us wanted to argue with him. Frankly, I don't think any of us wished to be on the field anymore, but Clover didn't want to hear those words. "No, if you are going to fight, we will do it together. I can't let you get hurt again! I'm not going to lose you again, goddamn it!" Clover yelled to the very tall and slanderous being.

"I need you alive, Clover. It would be suicide if I let you stay out here with me. Now go. I promise I will return to you safe and unharmed," Iviny put his wooden hand on Clover's face.

"I will go tell the others. You guys, go find a place to hide," I said, then ran to the others shouting.

"Get off the field! Get off the field now!"

They looked back at me, confused but stopping at once. I watched Darwin fall to his side as the shadows came back into his body. Wasma and Rocket helped pick up Darwin's limp body from the ground. Soon enough, MariGold, Acorn, and Moss ran in our direction, with the other three close behind, and the Sirens, including Cyrus, drove back into the water. After finding where Clover and Ruby were hiding, we hid behind some bushes far from the field.

Once we sat down, Wasma put Darwin's head on her lap for him to rest, black wisps of air still coming from his eyes.

"So that's Peep?" Moss asked, her hand interlocked with Ruby's.

"Yes, I assume it's part of a life cycle, Trollian to Tree Guardian," Ruby explained.

"Hush! I want to see what happens next," Rocket shushed them.

I peered through the bushes, wanting to see what Iviny would do. A crowd of soldiers swarmed him, but he used his arms to guard himself, slashing them in all directions. I could hear him speaking, but I had no clue what he was saying. He spoke louder and louder, chanting out something I believe to be in Treen. A blue hue pulsed from Iviny the louder he spoke. The chanting gave me a tight feeling in my chest. What was he going to do? No one has mentioned the powers of a Tree Guardian before this, but it's safe to assume I will witness it firsthand.

Chapter 19
Is It Really Time?

The blue hue around Iviny glowed stronger, and just like that, a whip of light spread from him.

"Everyone heads down now!" Wasma commanded. I didn't waste a second to do so. My head rushed between my knees, and my arms over my head. This, weirdly enough, reminded me of all those drills we did in school, but those weren't real. This was.

Even though I knew in my heart that I wouldn't get hurt, my life flashed before my eyes. Memories of being home with Father and even Mama. The times I was scared of lighting-yes, that's what this felt like, curling up in a ball in my closet because of the bad lightning that made us lose power. I wish Father were here to comfort me. I'm scared. I've been so frightened the whole time here. The last thing I wanted to do this summer was do anything like this; it was never a thought.

The light Iviny whipped spread through the lands. His power hit everything in its sight. The dead forest looked alive again, the battlefield that was once crimson turned back to dirt brown, and flowers started growing everywhere. The Center had been reborn. Even when there is happiness, there is always another side to it. When the magic from Iviny hit the Humans, they vanished into thin air. The Tree Guardian was the magician, and the soldiers were the assistants, but instead of reappearing, they were gone, hopefully forever.

After the magic passed us, we got up from behind the bushes. Clover was the first to rush over to Iviny.

"Oh, Iviny, you saved us!" Clover squealed.

"No, if it weren't for all of you, we'd probably never see an end to this fight. You were the ones who did the most. So, I thank you, not just from the Tree Guardians and Elders but from the colonies' people and creatures, as well as Peep," Iviny said.

Without a thought running through her mind, Clover wrapped her arms around Iviny, "Even if you aren't Peep anymore, you have its memories and our adventures. No matter what you say, you are my friend."

Iviny put his root hand on the top of her head. "I know, my dear," he began, "Peep truly loved and cared for you like a sister. I feel it still inside, its emotions, and its everything. Though I am not Peep, I will still be your friend."

A tear rolled down my face. The rest of us joined Clover in hugging Iviny. Some wept, some didn't. We needed this moment of domestic bliss after this long journey. The war had ended, and we likely all missed home, even if home wasn't the best place to be.

When we finally let go of each other, Iviny spoke once again. "Children, Union Beria is healing itself as we speak. Everyone can go home now when they are ready. You all must rest and heal with our land." Iviny then looked at Rocket, Moss, and me. "That goes for you three, too. If you would like, I can open a portal for you to return to your realm."

I nodded, stepping back from Iviny, "Yes, we would love that."

We separated to give Iviny room to make the portal and open it. I turned around and walked a couple of feet away from the others to take a final look at this beautiful place. That's when I felt someone grab my shoulder; it was Rocket. Before I could even say hi, he let a waterfall of words out.

"Cricket, I feel pride being here, and I feel like I have a chance and the courage to tell you something," he took a deep breath. That's when the waterfall part of his speech caught me off guard. He started to ramble in Russian with words I didn't know, and even if I did, he spoke way too quickly.

"Woah, woah, slow your roll, Rocket Man. I can't understand what you are saying," I grinned at him with soft eyes.

"I can't say it another way. You—you make me feel—" Rocket's words clashed together. "You make me happy, Cricket. And what I'm trying to say is that I really like you, and it's more than just in a friendly way. I love you, Cricket. You have meant the world to me for many years. Even if you don't feel the same way, I just needed to get it off my chest."

My body froze in place. Rocket likes me. No, he *loves* me. My brain felt like it was on autopilot as if someone turned it off and on again. Why would he like me? Am I dreaming? Was the last hour or so a dream? This could be the only explanation for it.

Rocket waved his hand in front of my face. I brought myself back to reality, staring into his doe-gray eyes. "You like me?"

"For the past couple of years, yes," he rubbed his neck.

I couldn't help myself from giggling and smiling at the thought that this was real. "Oh, Rocket, I love you too, and yes, in more than just a friend way."

We stood there in shock for a bit, still trying to figure out what to do now. Rocket moved his hand into mine. I couldn't help but stare into his eyes and glance down at his lips. Our faces inched closer to each other.

"Crick, may I?" Rocket began to ask.

"Yes," I blurted out. "I mean, if you want to, then yes." Why am I so awkward? I can't be normal for one second, can I? I did say I needed to learn to zipper my mouth shut.

The brightness of his smile shut my thoughts up quickly. Usually, I hate eye contact, but I could get lost in his eyes forever if I stared too long. My heart starts to flutter a mile a minute. Rocket grabbed my face gently and placed a kiss on my lips. The world felt like it had only us in it. Nothing around me mattered other than the feeling of Rocket's hands cupping my face and his lips on mine, kissing me. I swear my heart stopped for a moment. I kissed back, of course, with my arms wrapped around his neck. I might not get to do this often when we get home, so I want to savor this feeling for as long as possible. Rocket's lips were soft, and his kisses were gentle. I was floating from each kiss he gave me.

His face was bright pink when our lips separated, and I knew mine was, too.

"Sorry if I'm not the best," Rocket was about to start rambling.

"No, I liked it! Honestly, I've never kissed anyone before," I laughed, then kissed his cheek to reassure him.

"Good to know I don't suck," the smile I loved was glued on his face.

Something felt lighter. Maybe it was the air, or the weight of nervousness lifted off my chest. Whatever it was, my body finally felt at peace.

"I've liked you for a long time too. It's just at home; it's not the best place to like other boys, but here it feels different," I mentioned.

"Exactly! I would have kissed you long ago if I could," Rocket replied.

I turned my head to see Moss as she awed at us. Her hands were to her chin, intertwined together. "Finally! I've been waiting for this moment for years!" Moss skipped over to Rocket and me and gave us hugs.

"Oh, hush. We both were waiting for a long time, too," I snickered back. Rocket chuckled, which made all three of us laugh.

The moment was cut short when Iviny called us over. "Pures, the portal is ready. Are you ready to go home?"

I looked over to where everyone else was. Clover had her arms locked with Wasma as she leaned on her for support. MariGold, Ruby, and Acorn stood together, and Darwin, who had gained the energy to stay awake now, was standing next to his friends, smiling at me. I nodded to Iviny, grabbed my friends' hands, and walked back to the group.

Iviny spoke like a president talking during a speech, "Thank you for helping our home. Your work here is done. You three will forever be known as heroes in the colonies."

I looked through the warping portal. I could see the forest on the other side, *home.* Turning back to the group, we hugged and said our goodbyes.

As I hugged Darwin, he whispered, "See, everything worked out for you in the end. I wish you luck with him."

"Thank you. I hope things work out for you, too," I replied, letting go of him.

"She has someone that will love her more than I could," Darwin said, both of us turning our heads to see Wasma with Clover, "If she is happy, then I am happy too. That's all I ask for." Darwin looked back at me, "I hope we can meet again. Maybe one day you can show us around LongEdge, or maybe you could come back here? I could show you around properly without running for our lives." Darwin spoke out loud now.

"Of course! Only if it's possible. Is it possible?" I asked Iviny.

"Yes, it is. You still have a portal in your forest. All you have to do is ask for Mourn, and she will appear with it. The same goes for your powers. You will have them forever, even in your realm." He explained.

"That's good to know. Well, we should get going then. Our parents are probably worried sick," Rocket said. He grabbed my hand, and I grabbed Moss's as we stepped before the entrance back home.

I turned to look at my best friends. I could see Rocket was happy to go home, but when I looked at Moss, I couldn't tell her emotions.

"Are you okay, Moss?"

"Yeah, I'll be fine," her voice was low and distant.

"Moss, tell me what's wrong, please?"

Her glossy eyes looked guiltily at the ground. "Cricket," she paused. "I was talking to Ruby when you and Rocket were having a small making-out session, and I don't think I want to go home yet."

My mouth dropped, "What? Why would you not want to go back home?"

"I don't know. Since we came here, I have just had this feeling in my heart that I'm supposed to be here. No one here is the same as the next, and people here feel safer to be around than those asshole Humans. I was thinking that if I were here, I wouldn't have to fear walking home alone or people judging me for being me. I can't walk through that portal back home, Cricket," Moss said, looking me in the eyes.

"What about us, your parents, your sister, Judy, and your older brother, Isaiah? You can't leave us like this, Moss. We are your family," I cried out to her.

"Iviny said you can always visit me, and I can always come and visit, too. I can go and see my family whenever I want, and I won't be hurting myself mentally by living there anymore. I suffer because of others. Though my parents see me, no one else does."

"Then we will make them see you and hear you."

"I don't want to wait around for thirty years for people not to want to kill me if that were to even happen in the future. I'm a transgender woman—a black transgender woman. The world doesn't see me as a human to begin with. Maybe it was good that I was born as a Pure because I can have a better life here. I'm happy here, Cricket. I feel wanted and normal here. I've never felt that way in our realm, only with you guys. And I think I've fallen in love too. So please understand I just want to feel like I belong somewhere."

"What if you forget about us? What if you never want to see us again?" Rocket whispered, sounding in pain.

"Of course not! You guys will forever be my best friends. Rocket, you guys are the most unforgettable people I have ever met," she pleaded, "Though we won't see each other often, I'll always keep you with me. Also, who knows, I likely will get homesick in a matter of days and come rushing back into your arms."

Moss began to cry, "This isn't goodbye for us. It's just a *see you later*." She took a deep breath, "And when you get back home, can you tell my parents about everything and tell them they are amazing for what they have done for me through these years? Tell them that I love them oh so very much, please?"

I wiped Moss's tears, "Of course, *Mossie Mow.*"

"And make sure Judy has a good life, and maybe you could bring her here one day? She will believe you guys, trust me," Moss continued.

"I will look after her like a hawk for you," Rocket sniffled.

"I know you will, Rocket. Also," she wipes her cheek, "You better treat Cricket well because if I find out you crushed his heart, I will come and find you and crush a lot more than that. Do you hear me?"

"Yes, ma'am,"

"Alright then. I'll see you later, Rocket Man, Camel Cricket. Go back home, and don't forget to visit me," she said, taking another deep breath.

"I don't think we will ever forget to visit you," I said.

No surprise, we all cried as we held each other for the last time, but we had to leave at some point.

So we walked into that portal, Rocket's hand in one of mine and an empty hand where Moss should have been. Tears ran down my face as we left. We exited the portal, and we were now back to our realm. I watched as the warped light slowly left my view and closed.

"I guess we should go find our parents. We have some explaining to do, and we are probably in so much trouble," I choked at my words.

"We definitely are, but I'll be there with you the whole way," Rocket gave me a small peck on the lips and wiped my tears.

"Thanks, Rocket," I gave a small smile to the Russian boy beside me.

Hand in hand, we made our way to my house. Though we both knew that when it came time to tell Moss's parents and our parents everything, they wouldn't believe our journey, but it would be the truth. My heart felt like it was ripping the farther we walked away from where the entrance of Union Beria was. I'll never forget Moss or the colonies, even if I tried. She will always be my best friend, and the colonies are a form of second home to me now. Anyway, they aren't so far from us. We can still see each other when we wish, so why do I feel so depressed? Maybe the place and its people imprinted in me somehow, like how Mourn imprinted us with our symbols. It will never go away. Life will be different without seeing Moss every day, with our new powers and the markings on our hands that are forever branded on our palms.

The adventures and the fight- even if I didn't want to do it at first- I don't want to forget it happened. All I know is that the memories will constantly flow through me, like the *river in the meadow.*

'The End.'

July 16th, 1985

Chapter 20
The Phone Call

2:09 pm; Tuesday, July 16th, 1985

Gregory picked up the house phone and called his ex-wife, Catherine. She had called him at work earlier that day regarding having Cricket come up to Queens for her wedding.

"Gregory, I'm sorry I had to call your work today. I know your job is...significant—so significant that I had to find out your workplace number from our lawyer." Catherine had sat on the couch with her cordless phone.

"I don't know why that is of any importance to you." Greg had taken his glasses off and set them on the counter.

"It is when you are working for the government, Greg. Are you working with the Army again?"

"Why do I need to answer that question? It is absolutely ridiculous."

"You are, aren't you? Since our marriage, I've been telling you something isn't right with them. I thought you stopped that line of work for Cricket."

"And I thought you stopped drinking for Cricket, too."

"Those are two different things, Gregory."

"Is it, though?"

"I only started drinking when you left for that fucking job! What do you think it was like being pregnant while your husband was across the world working for bastards!"

"Don't blame your fuck ups on me!"

"*My*- no, I am done with talking about the past. I have worked my ass off trying to get better. Do you know how many years I've been drug clean for? Five years. In those five years, I have attended over a hundred AA meetings, and I *still* attend them." Catherine choked out, trying to breathe and not cry. "Now, can we please talk about why I called you to begin with?"

"Yes."

"Thank you. As I said earlier, I am getting remarried, and I want Cricket to be there. As for our agreement with the courts, I am legally allowed to see Cricket once I got help, and I have. I don't ask much from you these days. I just want to see my son."

"Catherine-"

"I rarely drink anymore; when I do, it's only one glass for a special occasion. If you don't believe me, I can fax you my paperwork."

"There is no need for that." Greg looks at the ceiling, "He doesn't like you. You do know that, right?"

"I know. He can hate me all he wants, and yes, my biases haven't changed, but you know how guilty I feel about what I did that day. I hate myself for what I did and live with that guilt daily."

"Cricket does too..."

Catherine goes silent, her hand over her mouth, and tears roll down her face. "What do I have to do to see my son? I only want to see him for a week or two. I want him to meet his new family."

Gregory walks over to the back door. He looks through it to see Cricket on the tire swing reading. "Fine."

"Fine?" Catherine was surprised by this response.

"You can take Cricket. You can even take him for the summer."

"What?"

"You heard me."

"That's- Greg, thank you!"

"You're still a bitch for everything else, and he won't be happy one bit."

"I know." She stopped to think, "Wait, what is the catch, though?

"I have a job opportunity and I won't be home to care for him if I'm out of the country."

"The Army called you, didn't they, Lieutenant Mont?"

"Yeah, they did."

"To where?"

"It's classified."

"Bullshit. If I am taking Cricket for the summer, I want to know where his father will be."

Greg sighs, "I'm stationed in a place called *Union Beria.*"

"Oh? I've never heard of such a place. Does Cricket know?"

"No, but I will have him call you later so you can talk to him. All I ask of you is not to tell him anything about the trip."

"I promise."

"Good. I'll get a ticket for the flight in the morning before work, and he'll be in your arms by no later than tomorrow evening. I am putting all my trust in you, Catherine. And that is a lot of trust coming from me."

"You have no idea how happy I am right now! Thank you, Greg."

"Goodbye."

He hangs up the phone, leaving her phone line beeping. Catherine doesn't know how to feel. On the one hand, she is excited to have her son in her grasp after almost eight years, and on the other, she is scared about Greg's job as Lieutenant Mont, going to Union Beria without his son knowing.